"Allergy Shots
is one of those non-stop
reading experiences.
It takes you by the throat
and never lets go.
And, at the end of the book,
you're left with the
chilling question
of where the truth stopped
and the fiction began."

Dick Case
Columnist
Syracuse Herald-Journal,
and *Herald American*

**A masterful integration of
medical and police intrigue;
an absorbing, shocking, uplifting
and riveting story.**
Rabbi Dr. Reuven P. Bulka
Ottawa, Ontario, Canada

**Allergy Shots grabbed me
and dragged me into the
shocking underworld of medicine. It
fills the prescription
for action and suspense.**
Anne Richter, Producer/Anchor
WWNY-TV, Watertown, New York

**Clever interweaving
of medical practice, mayhem,
and mystery.**
Howard M. Spiro, MD
Professor of Medicine
Yale University School of Medicine

1 May 2000

To Dianne K. Kubis,

With my warm regards,

Rob Liw

ALLERGY SHOTS

A NOVEL OF MEDICAL SUSPENSE BY
ROBERT B. LITMAN

IVY LEAGUE PRESS

All inquiries should be addressed to the Publisher, Ivy League Press, Inc., P.O. Box 1192, Ogdensburg, New York 13669 (TEL. (315) 393-7600; FAX (315) 393-3873)

This is a work of fiction. The characters, names, incidents, places and dialogue are products of the author's imagination, and are not to be construed as real.

Cover Design by Kenneth Hine

LIBRARY OF CONGRESS CATALOGUE #92-70081

ISBN #0-918921-04-X
FIRST EDITION, JANUARY, 1993
Third printing, March, 1993
Printed in the United States of America
12 11 10 9 8 7 6 5 4 3

For Niki,
who lingered for a time,
drawn tenaciously towards
the dark doors of that other place,
then came back
to the kids and to me.

FOREWORD

There is nothing more frustrating or baffling than a coroner's or medical examiner's autopsy which turns up nothing—a negative autopsy. Dr. Rob Litman is aware of this and uses it to embark on a yarn which is replete with forensic allusions and medical facts, some of the latter just recently discovered.

The tale of a brilliant neurosurgeon teamed with a hard-bitten cop following a tortuous trail, beginning with a seemingly negative autopsy and ending with a surprise denouement, holds the reader's interest from beginning to end. The author displays a wide acquaintanceship with immunology, allergies and pathology, and laces his entertaining and fast-moving story with this scientific know-how. He also knows the slang commonly used in coroners' offices and this adds spice here and there in the book.

Dr. Litman graduated from Yale University and is a family physician and allergist. He has a flourishing and busy practice, and yet still finds time to write. This, his third book, a suspenseful mixture of who-dun-it and forensic knowledge, will keep the reader turning the pages and always fascinated.

Hugh F. Frame, M.D.
St. Lawrence County Coroner
Morristown, New York

PROLOGUE

19 August **Three Years Ago**, *Syracuse, New York*

Patricia Benham, resident superintendent of the Fairdale Arms, mouthed the last bite of her veal cutlet, while glancing absently at the small TV screen. She watched Dwight Gooden strike out Jack Clark, then switched it off and headed for her apartment door. Letting her cat in just after supper was a daily ritual. She knew that Josh would be curled up on the lawn near the clump of junipers.

He was.

Patricia opened the outside door. Josh brushed by her, but instead of racing directly to her apartment, he paused in the vestibule, tilting his head, eyeing the ceiling, sampling the air. Josh proceeded cautiously to the door of 1-C, sat on its threshold and meowed.

It was then that Patricia noticed the odd smell. Sniffing, she approached her cat and wondered

1

what stimulus had drawn him to the door of Dr. Natalie Lepert's apartment. *What is that awful smell?* she asked herself. *Is that why Josh is acting crazy? Is the stink coming from in there?*

Patricia knocked on the door. While waiting for an answer, she acknowledged that she knew very little about the young female pathologist—only that she worked at the new EconoMed Clinic in central Syracuse, entertained infrequently and was a model tenant. Not getting any response to her knocking, Patricia pressed the lighted button on the jamb. In the distance, on the other side of the door, she heard the faint hum of the bell. Somehow—Patricia did not know why—the awful stench became stronger.

A profusion of thoughts rushed through her head. *Am I closer? Is that why it smells worse? Did the doctor leave some meat out? It's been in the eighties— maybe she didn't turn her air conditioner on?* She pressed the buzzer again, then again.

Patricia Benham went to her apartment and fetched her passkeys, then returned to 1-C. She knocked and rang—there was still no answer. She inserted the key into the lock, turned it and opened the door.

The swamp-stink of death assaulted her. Shaking, Patricia was frozen in the doorway. She peered into the dark foyer of apartment 1-C. Then, fighting overwhelming nausea, compelled by a force she could not comprehend, she followed her nose into the darkness, through the living room, into the bedroom — the clear origin of the aroma.

Patricia flicked on the wall light. She spotted the porcelain vase tipped over by the window. She noticed the plant on its side on the nightstand table, brown earth spilled. She saw the partially decomposed body of Dr. Natalie Lepert lying under the covers, flies dancing on her bloated face, a white sheet tucked neatly under her chin.

Patricia ran out of the apartment and vomited recently chewed veal cutlet onto the marble vestibule floor.

The smell did not seem to bother Detective Captain Bertram Hollister, Syracuse P.D. He moved swiftly from one side of the crime scene to the other. He stopped at the foot of the bed, shook his head repeatedly and tapped his left thumb on his black notebook.

"What's the matter, Captain?" asked the forensic man who was in the process of vacuuming the carpet for fibers.

Hollister scratched his thick gray hair. "Tell me, Eddie, do you buy a suicide?"

"That's the way it looks. I bet when the ME cracks her open, he finds her full of some sort of shit."

The seasoned detective thought, *The scene's too perfect.*

"Whatcha thinking, Captain?" asked the forensic man.

"It'll be in my report," he said.

CHAPTER 1

21 April **Present Day**

Dr. Isaac Darnell drove his Yale blue Chevy Suburban off the Northeast Extension of the Pennsylvania Turnpike onto Interstate-81 North. He glanced at the sign which said: *Scranton 12, Binghamtom 72, Syracuse 150* and he smiled. From his study of the map he knew that his destination, a place called Ogdensburg, was 130 miles from Syracuse. He did some rapid mental calculations, then thought, *I'll be there in about six hours. I wonder what this lady's going to be like.*

Darnell sped through the cool spring morning, only marginally concentrating on his driving. Much as he tried to do otherwise, he continued to dwell on the most horrible twelve seconds of his life, playing and replaying them over and over again in his mind.

He was seated with his wife and two daughters

at the head table in the main ballroom of the Bellevue-Stratford Hotel in downtown Philadelphia. This was to be his night, the dinner in his honor thrown by the Philadelphia County Medical Society.

Vinny Parisi came out dressed as a waiter, set his tray down and began firing. Six shots. Two into Darnell's chest. He remembered leaping at the man, but in vain. One shot each into the heads of Marilyn, Laurel and Cindy Darnell—at close range. Darnell recalled looking up from the floor and seeing Parisi mouthing the barrel and killing himself. Then, as he was recovering, he saw the headlines: **DERANGED PATIENT KILLS BLACK NEUROSURGEON'S FAMILY, WOUNDS DOCTOR**.

Isaac Darnell wiped away his tears. He put on his turn signal, then took Exit 48 of I-81. An hour later he stopped the Suburban in front of a huge white brick home on a quiet street in a town called Ogdensburg, New York. He withdrew an envelope from his pocket and checked the address on the door. "This is it," he said aloud.

Darnell was a huge black man in his mid-fifties who appeared to most, not as a respected, renowned neurosurgeon, but as an ex-player of some professional sport. His hair was steel gray and cropped short, his skin the color of caramel. His eyes were large, glistening and liquid brown and they flanked a small, thrice-broken nose. His thick, well-muscled body made you think of an O.J. Simpson or a Larry Holmes, but his finely manicured mustache, pearly teeth, thin lips and stunningly tailored, gray pin-striped three piece suit made you reconsider and peg him for a professional.

He mounted the steps and pressed the doorbell.

Darnell heard the knob turn, then peered into the regal face of an elegant woman in her sixties. He saw both strength and sadness.

"I am Dr. Darnell."

"I've been expecting you, Doctor. I am Sophie Lepert. Please come in."

The woman led him through a high, well-lit front hall into an ornate sitting room where she beckoned him to sit opposite her on matching brocaded Queen Anne chairs. He felt the cold stare of her green eyes sweep over his face and body, then heard her say, "I should like to get right to the point, Doctor."

"By all means."

"Why did you answer my advertisement?"

Darnell reviewed in his mind the ad he had seen four months ago in the "Physician, other, wanted" section of the classifieds of *The New England Journal of Medicine*:

Intelligent, curious & honest doctor needed to conduct medicolegal investigation. Full time. Term: up
to one year. Fee: $1,000,000. Send complete c.v. to:
c/o Journal, Box 68A.

Darnell lounged back in his chair and stroked
his chin, silent.

"Unfair question?" asked Sophie Lepert.

"No," he replied without hesitancy, "but I suspect that you know from my resumé that I am a
retired neurosurgeon."

"You are correct," she said dryly, "but there are
many retired physicians. Why did you leave
practice?"

(six shots)

He perceived the raw desire for truth in her
eyes and he told her . . . "and now Mrs. Lepert, I
should like to know why you have chosen me.
Others certainly must have approached you?"

"I have not employed you yet, Dr. Darnell—this
is merely an interview." She paused, collecting her
thoughts. "But yes, you are right. I have had more
than a thousand replies and have interviewed
nearly a hundred people." She was silent for thirty
seconds, then: "Do you know what *chutzpah*
means?"

Darnell smiled and nodded.

"I am a Jew; I use such words."

"It's a good word."

"Do you have it, Doctor?"

Darnell's mind flashed back to the days just after his graduation from high school, when he would climb into the ring of one South Philly gym or other and stare viciously, sweat streaming from his face, at his opponent. His heart would race when the announcer said: "And here in the blue corner wearing gold trunks is Ike 'The Iron Man' Darnell, DarNELL!" He would listen to the applause of the crowd, flex his muscles, dance up and down and loose violent, whistling blows into the air in the general direction of the other boxer. His trainer, Benny Goldman, would sit him in his corner just before the opening bell, slap his face hard and say: "*Chutzpah*, Ike—give me *chutzpah*" and he would rise to his feet and try to beat the other man senseless.

Darnell's eyes met hers. "Yes, Mrs. Lepert. In my own way, I do."

"But you don't *need* the money." A statement.

"No."

Sophie Lepert smiled timidly. "I believe you are the right man."

"I have not accepted. I should like you to explain to me what you meant in your letter by 'a family investigation.' Does it regard your husband?"

Lepert's eyes misted. "My daughter, Natalie. She was a doctor, a pathologist in Syracuse."

"*Was?*"

"She died almost three years ago. I believe she was murdered. I want you, Dr. Darnell, to find out who killed her, why and how."

(six shots)

He fingered his vest just over the thick scar below his left nipple. "Call me Ike," he said.

CHAPTER 2

29 April

Ike Darnell drove slowly through the hamlets of St. Lawrence and Jefferson Counties en route to I-81, the highway to Syracuse. In his extraordinary mind he sorted the bits and pieces he knew of the life and death of Dr. Natalie Lepert. He had spent more than a week poring over documents with Sophie Lepert, learning all that he could from that savvy lady. Those papers now filled two briefcases stored in the locked compartment in the rear of the Suburban. Fifty thousand dollars in tens, twenties, fifties and hundreds filled a third. *For expenses, bribes and so on*, Sophie had said.

Ike was most intrigued by the autopsy report which had failed to reveal the cause of death. Some bruises were found at the base of her neck and some hemorrhages in her eyes—otherwise it was completely negative. *Consistent with strangulation,* he thought, *but there was no evidence of a struggle and no definite trauma to the trachea, so asphyxiation is unlikely.* He remembered that the brain, heart, lungs, and other internal organs were all found to be grossly and microscopically normal. Toxicology tests for drugs and alcohol were similarly negative. So the sovereign question in Ike's mind was: What killed Natalie Lepert?

Ike ran over an already dead porcupine, turned onto the highway and mulled over the reason why Sophie Lepert was *certain* that her daughter was murdered: *It was in David's diary!* she had told him.

Ike learned that David Lepert had graduated from Harvard Law during the Great Depression. *A pity*, thought Ike, whose own college and med school alma mater had been Yale. There followed more than fifty years of legal practice in tiny Ogdensburg, three wives, but only one child—Natalie. He had become ill in the two years before his daughter's death with an undiagnosable form of leukemia and Natalie had come to visit with him almost every weekend. After one of those visits—two months before her death—he had scrupulously recorded in his diary: *Natalie is certain that she is in danger. She feels that her life is threatened.* Unfortunately, at that time, David Lepert's Alzheimer's Syndrome was progressing rapidly; he never mentioned this information to his wife or to anyone else. Sophie had found the diary in his safe three months after David's death, two years after Natalie's. Shortly after, she had hired attorneys to reopen the case at the Onondaga County DA's office. These efforts had failed. Then, she had placed her advertisement.

The other salient fact in Ike's mind was difficult for him to comprehend—the signature on the autopsy report. A Dr. Harold Hutchins, Natalie Lepert's colleague and boss at the EconoMed Clinic, was an assistant county Medical Examiner; he had done the post-mortem!

Nearing Syracuse, he tried to free his thoughts of these details and concentrate on the tasks he had chosen for his first day in the field. Soon he reached a calm, a sense of well-being, of anxious anticipation, only to have it shattered by the visual image of a bullet emerging from his younger daughter's left temple, of her brain tissue spattering a shrimp cocktail.

Ike stopped on a quiet tree-lined street on the outskirts of the city, exited from his vehicle and walked up the sidewalk to the front door of the Fairdale Arms, a three-story, red brick garden apartment complex which he surmised rented only to Yuppies and well-to-do seniors. He studied the black name plates on the panel by the door, then pressed the button next to "Benham, P. (super)."

"Yes?" was the staticky response through the small, circular speaker.

"Mrs. Benham," he said into the microphone. "My name is Darnell. I would like to speak with you about Dr. Natalie Lepert."

A pregnant silence. Ike heard birds chirping and bees humming. Then the buzzer rang and he opened the heavy metal door. He stopped in the foyer in front of a floor to ceiling mirror and checked the knot of his dark blue tie, seeing that it contrasted nicely with his white shirt and charcoal gray suit. He knocked on the door of Apartment 1-A and was admitted seconds later.

Ike noted that Patricia Benham was a polished, neatly dressed woman in her early forties. He drank in the short, frosted, permed hair, the patrician features, the ruffled white silk blouse and the neatly pressed brown slacks.

"The police have my full statement," she said before directing him to a chair. "Why are you here, Mr. uh . . . ?"

Ike had read that statement. "Darnell. Isaac Darnell. I have been hired by Dr. Lepert's mother to investigate her death."

"I see. What can I possibly know that would be important?"

"Do you think she was murdered, Mrs. Benham?"

"There was talk of that in the press; mostly, I think, to sell papers." She looked into Ike's eyes and was struck by their intensity. "No, I think she killed herself."

"How?" he asked laconically.

Patricia Benham shrugged her shoulders.

"Did you ever see her with guests in her apartment?"

"Dr. Lepert was a *very* private person. If she had visitors here, I never saw them. Occasionally, in the summers, I would see her sitting by the pool— always alone. She would take a dip, towel off, then bury her nose in a paperback or a magazine. Twenty minutes later I'd look up and she'd be gone."

"Did she have friends here in the apartments?"

"None that I knew of."

"You are the superintendent, are you not?"

Patricia nodded. "For the past eight years."

"Did Dr. Lepert have much contact with you?"

"Seldom," she said. "Usually mundane stuff—a stopped-up toilet, rattle in the air conditioner; that kind of thing."

Ike sensed that Patricia Benham was being honest with him, was holding nothing back. He arose from his chair. "I appreciate your time, ma'am. Do you have any objection to my speaking with others who live here?"

"Not at all."

"Good day, Mrs. Benham." He left, then strolled down the corridor and knocked on the next door. A tiny elderly woman opened the door a crack, chain on.

"Excuse me, ma'am. I'd like to speak with you about Dr. Lepert."

"I don't know nothing," she shrieked before slamming the door.

During the next forty minutes Ike questioned six other people. He learned nothing.

Out on the sidewalk, while returning to his car, he spotted a middle-aged, black mailman, approaching the door from which Ike had gone out. He was sweating briskly under the weight of his heavy bag. "Excuse me, sir. Do you have a moment?"

Relieved to unshoulder his sack, if only for a short time, the man stopped and said, "What can I do for you?"

"Does the name, Dr. Natalie Lepert, mean anything to you?"

"Sure does. Apartment 1-C. It was a tragedy, ya know."

"Yes, it was. Did you ever see her with anybody else?"

"Sure did. You from the police?"

"No, I am conducting a private investigation into her death. Do you remember any details?"

"Yep. Twice I had to deliver certified letters to her—ya know, knock on her door, get her signature and so forth."

"And?"

"And both times I saw the same guy in her place, usually sitting there in the living room drinking coffee."

"Did that man have a name?" asked Ike excitedly.

"Must've, but I didn't know it. But he was one strange looking dude—not the kind you'd forget."

"How so?"

"His ear. I think it was the left one. Mangled, like a bunch of scar tissue—sorta like the shape of a regular ear, but all scarred up. His other ear was fine. A man doesn't forget something like that."

Pinnal reconstruction, thought Ike. *Probably born without an ear or lost it accidentally and had plastic surgery.* "Can you describe him otherwise?"

"Never saw him standin, so's I can't guess his height, but he was medium build, white, partially balding, probably in his late thirties, dressed in blue overalls both times. Never spoke to me, but he seemed friendly enough."

"Did you ever see him since?"

The postman shook his head.

Ike Darnell was ecstatic. In all the documents he had reviewed, there was no mention of such a man. "One more question."

"Shoot."

"Did you tell the police about this guy?"

"They never asked," he replied.

Ike climbed into his Suburban and drove into downtown Syracuse hoping that he would have no trouble finding the EconoMed Clinic.

Sophie's directions proved to be accurate. He parked in a huge, drive-in, six story garage which was connected by a belt-driven walkway over a small street to the main clinic building. Arriving in the futuristic lobby—thirty foot high, hanging op-sculptures, walls of silvers, reds and bright blues— Ike approached a stunning receptionist: "Excuse me, miss?"

"Yes, sir," she said, soft and sultry, "Just how may I help you?"

"I'd like to see Dr. Harold Hutchins. Would you direct me to his office?"

"Is the doctor expecting you?"

"No."

"Your name?"

"Darnell. Dr. Isaac Darnell."

She lifted the telephone and tapped a four digit code. After a brief conversation, she hung up, turned towards Ike and said, "I'm sorry, but Dr. Hutchins is extremely busy now. Would you care to make an appointment?"

Ike leaned his face over the counter, his lips three inches from the entirely too pretty blond. He slipped into his West Philly down-home jive talk. "Now you lissen up, chile. You call dat honkey back and ast him when he wants ta talk ta me bout Natalie Lepert. You DIG?"

She re-called, then smiled primly at Ike, her face a mask. "Dr. Darnell, Dr. Hutchins' office is on the eleventh floor. Take elevator number six over there. He is expecting you right now."

Ike Darnell allowed her a wide, toothy grin, then moved away without a word.

Sitting across the desk from him, Ike studied Harold Hutchins and his elegant office. The man was as tall as Ike—nearly six-four—but slim and bony. He had a pinched face, a stubby nose helmeted by thick black horn-rims, curly brown-gray hair and vacant hazel eyes.

On the walls Ike saw dozens of Perma-plaqued diplomas which clung to thick damask wallpaper. Inlaid on the highly varnished, cherry desk was a porcelain rectangle, flanked by gilt-framed photographs of a pinch-faced woman and three teenagers. Ike waited. Finally, Hutchins finished his phone conversation, set down the receiver, then thrust his hands into the pockets of his long white coat and said affably: "Dr. Darnell, how may I be of service to you? Something about Dr. Lepert I understand?"

Ike straightened his spine and leaned forward. "Precisely. I have been hired by Dr. Lepert's mother to investigate the circumstances of her death. You posted her, didn't you?"

The corners of Hutchins' mouth quivered for an instant. "Correct. If you know that, then you must also be aware that we never did determine the cause of death."

"Yes, I read your report thoroughly. What I want to know is: what was your gut reaction? Setting the lack of medical evidence aside, why do you think she died?"

"You want a speculation?"

"Yes."

"Probably natural causes." He reclined in his chair. "We found nothing, but she died. Ergo, she had to have had a lethal cardiac rhythm disturbance. For some damned reason, she went into ventricular fibrillation, her heart stopped and she stopped breathing."

Ike stared at his forehead and saw the beads of sweat. "You say 'we,' Dr. Hutchins. Did another doctor assist you with the autopsy? It wasn't recorded as such."

"No. You're right. I was alone—just using the editorial 'we.'" Hutchins pursed his lips and placed his elbows on the porcelain inlay. Ike saw that his fingertips were trembling.

"Didn't you find yourself presented with an ethical conflict, doctor, being asked to do an autopsy on a *colleague* of yours?" asked Ike, now leaning closer to the white-lipped pathologist. "Why didn't you excuse yourself for that reason? Surely you're not the only medical examiner in Syracuse?"

Hutchins sucked in his breath. "She hired you, you say?" he countered, not answering.

"Yes, Mrs. Sophie Lepert believes that her daughter was murdered. She retained me to find out how and by whom."

Hutchins blew out his breath, rustling papers on the desktop. "That rich old bitch is nuts. Why now, after almost three years, is she digging up this crap?"

"I believe that that is her prerogative."

"What's your field, Darnell?" asked Hutchins in a voice devoid of charm or pretense.

"I used to be a neurosurgeon. Now I'm retired."

"You like this private eye stuff?"

Ike didn't respond. Hutchins went on: "All right. I'm willing to admit that it was possible that Natalie was killed. But, if so, the murderer was damned shrewd. There aren't too many causes of death that would slip through an intensive forensic post-mortem." Having regained some aplomb, Hutchins smiled.

Ike said, "True, but suppose something did?"

Hutchins chuckled. "Then it did and it's history."

"Did you kill her, doctor?" asked Ike.

The smile froze on Hutchins' face like a bizarre

21

theatre mask. He let out a roar of laughter, stood and said, "Well, well! It appears that dear Mrs. Lepert hired the perfect chap to conduct her precious investigation. You're about as subtle as a fart in a spacesuit. If you have no further questions, *doctor*, then I must be on my way. Need I show you the exit?"

Shortly after he saw the heavy door click behind the black man, Dr. Harold Hutchins reached into his bottom desk drawer and extracted a small, compact, jointed pearl-white telephone. He lifted the receiver and made a connection automatically with a like device in a walnut-walled den two thousand miles away. After two short rings, a man with a deep voice answered: "Yes?"

"It's Hutchins, sir. We may have a bit of trouble. . . ."

This conversation lasted eighteen minutes.

Ike Darnell sat on a chair between the two double beds in his room at the Syracuse Holiday Inn. On one bed he had emptied the contents of one of his briefcases; on the other were the remnants of a turkey club sandwich, french fries and a Coke. He glanced at his watch and saw that it was almost 6 PM. Sliding the chair closer to the nightstand, he lifted the telephone and dialed a number in Bryn Mawr, Pennsylvania—one that he knew quite well.

As the sibilant hums reverberated in his ear, he thought, *He owes me. I removed a tumor the size of a grapefruit from his little girl's brain—and she just graduated from Vassar. He'll help if he can.*

"Cohen residence," he heard through the receiver.

"Yes," said Ike. "I'd like to speak with Dr. Cohen. Please tell him it's Dr. Darnell."

"One moment." Then: "Ikey! How the hell are you?"

"Terrific, Hymie. Listen—I need a favor."

"You got it," said one of the preeminent plastic surgeons on the Philadelphia Main Line. "What can I do for you?"

"I'm doing some investigative work—you know, just to occupy my spare time."

"Peddling your learned ass for plaintiffs' attorneys in malpractice cases?"

"Not exactly," said Ike. "Anyhow, I seem to recall that you plastic boys have central computer listings somewhere regarding unusual reconstructive cases."

"Correct. The American Academy provides that service for research and referral purposes. What do you want to know?"

"Specifically, is there anyone in the central or northern New York area who gets a hard-on doing complete ears?"

"Pinnal reconstruction? Sure is. There's one

23

guy—he was a classmate of mine at Penn Med. His name's Jenkins, Ardus Jenkins—practices at Strong Memorial in Rochester. I saw him at the national meeting a couple of years ago. He presented a paper discussing almost twenty patients he had operated. He does a flap rotation procedure from the shoulder on the affected side. He swings this mass of skin, muscle and fat over to the side of the head, slips in a Silastic implant to take the place of the cartilage and fashions a decent looking external ear. The man's an artist."

"Anybody else in his area who does the same procedure?" asked Ike.

"Don't think so. That's his forte. He probably gets all the referrals that don't go to New York City. You got a specific patient in mind?"

"Yes and no. I can describe him, but I don't know his name. He probably lives in the general vicinity of Syracuse. His name, Hymie. I need to know his name. Can you run a computer check."

"Don't need the computer. Tell me what you've got. I'll call Jenkins. I saved his ass in med school more than once. He'll tell me if he knows."

"Great!" Ike recounted to Cohen the information he'd garnered from the postman at the Fairdale Arms and gave him his phone number.

"You stay put, Ikey. I'll get back to you. *Shalom*, my friend."

24

Ike pressed the cradle button, then called Sophie Lepert in Ogdensburg. "Sophie, it's Ike."

"Getting anywhere?" she asked.

"Possibly. Tell me—did Natalie have any boyfriends?"

"None that I knew of. She spent a good deal of time, though, with a high school classmate of hers. She's a local Ogdensburg girl who works as a broker for Shearson-Lehman-Hutton in Syracuse. I recall Natalie telling me that they would go to concerts together—things like that. Her name's Tracey Barr. She's listed in the book. Tell me what you've been up to."

Ike summarized his day's activities, noting details and his thoughts.

"You've got to watch Hutchins, Ike. There's something about that man I just don't like."

"I know what you mean. Sophie, how much do you know about the EconoMed Clinic?"

"A lot. It's the biggest HMO in New York and one of the most successful prepaid health plans in the country. They're a huge operation and burgeoning all the time. A few years ago they took over our little hospital here in Ogdensburg and put all of the local docs on their payroll. EconoMed is the future of medicine, certainly in these parts. My David was heavily invested in their stock—and Black Monday didn't even scratch their skin. It's a veritable gold mine."

Ike pondered these facts. "Thanks for the info, Sophie. I'm holed up in a Holiday Inn. I'll be in touch tomorrow. I've got a few leads—they may pan out."

"Talk to you then. And Ike?"

"Yes?"

"I want your opinion. Do you think my Natalie was murdered?"

Ike paused, then said, "I don't know, but I sure as hell am going to find out. Good night."

The ringing telephone awakened him. Ike snatched the receiver on the second ring. "Yes?"

"Ikey, it's Hymie. I think I've got your man. Jenkins has a home computer on which he stores all his patient records. He's done only two ears on males currently in their thirties or forties. One of them's a Puerto Rican. The other has to be the man you've described."

Ike grabbed his pad and pen. "Go ahead."

"The guy's name is Marvin Hambly. Lives at 124 Alden Street in Auburn, New York. Lost his left ear in a knife fight when he was a teenager. Jenkins did him in three stages about fifteen years ago. And that bit about the overalls fits. He's employed—or at least was, the last time Jenkins saw him—at an industrial scientific laboratory. He's a biologist or something. Am I helping you, Ikey?"

Ike finished writing. "You're terrific, my friend!"

"Good night then. I've got to be up early to make the noses of a couple of little ladies more presentable."

"Sleep well." Ike hung up the phone and looked at his watch: 11:05 PM—too late to call the man. He dialed Auburn information. Twenty seconds later he had the phone number of Marvin Hambly. *Auburn*, he thought. *It's less than hour from here.*

He slipped out of his clothes, washed up and climbed into bed.

Tomorrow, he thought before clicking off the lamp. *Tomorrow, Hambly'll be my second stop.*

CHAPTER 3

30 April

A thin kinky-haired man wearing silver-rimmed sunglasses watched the early morning sun poke through the haze which overlay the quiet city street. Unenthusiastically he tapped his right index finger on the steering wheel of his tan Pontiac roughly in time to the rock music on the radio.

Suddenly, he swept his hand to the dashboard and switched off the music. His eyes followed the burly black man's every movement — from the front door of the Holiday Inn to the parking lot across the road.

He started his engine and moved out behind the blue Suburban.

His journey was short. Eight blocks. He parked a half block from the Syracuse Police Department, noting the black man's entrance at 7:03 AM in his small spiral notebook.

Ike Darnell had no trouble connecting with Detective Captain Bertram Hollister. He had made one inquiry at the main desk, followed a uniformed cop down a wide corridor, then found himself shaking hands with a gray-haired, red-faced, short, thin man wearing a dark tweed sports jacket and chain-smoking unfiltered Camels. Ike was most impressed by Hollister's eyes—deep, dark and fiery, like embers in a campfire—and by his coarse, husky John Wayne voice.

"Coffee?" asked the detective.

"Please. Black."

Hollister poured two steaming cups from the pot next to his desk. "So what do you want to know about Dr. Natalie Lepert?"

"I'm working for Mrs. Lepert who believes Natalie was murdered."

Hollister stubbed out a Camel and lit another. Through the miasma of smoke Ike saw a gleam in the man's eyes.

Finally, after sipping deeply from his cup, Hollister spoke: "The diary bit?"

Ike nodded.

"As I am sure you know, Mrs. Lepert took that to the D.A. last year. She wanted him to reopen the investigation. The D.A. called me and asked my opinion." He paused.

"And what did you say?" asked Ike.

"On the one hand, I never did buy that suicide

30

or natural causes bullshit. On the other, I knew what we had come up with after more than a month on that case—not a fucking thing." He paused again and drank some coffee. "So I told the D.A. that if all Mrs. Lepert had was a diary entry by an old fart with brain damage, we would be wasting our time."

Ike was stunned. "Are you telling me, Captain Hollister, that you believe Dr. Lepert was murdered?"

"Yep. Some real smart cookie offed that girl. I knew it the moment I laid eyes on the scene in her bedroom. It was too goddamned perfect. It just looked too much like a healthy thirty year old woman went to bed naked one night and happened to die during her sleep. For thirty-five fucking years I've been finding stiffs and I never saw one that looked so . . . so set up."

"But you found no evidence."

"Correct," said Hollister. "We went over every inch of that place with fucking microscopes— including the doors, windows and the grounds. We found nothing. No evidence of break-in; no evidence of any other human being's presence in that apartment except for Natalie Lepert's."

"How about the autopsy, Captain? Do you remember why Hutchins was called to do it?"

"Sure do—and I thought it fucking odd right then and there, that very night when I was talking to him on the phone. I asked him why he didn't get somebody else to do it since he knew the victim. Do you know what he told me?"

Ike shook his head.

"He said that it was a fucking weekend and that he was the pathologist on call and that those were the rules. He lied on his report."

"Lied? How so?"

"He said he took vaginal smears for semen."

Ike's mind flashed to that page of the autopsy report. "Weren't they lost?"

"That's what Hutchins maintained. He says he took them, packed them off to the forensic lab, but that somebody over there mislaid them."

"Who's to know if he lied?" asked Ike. "He did the post alone."

"Not true," said Hollister, wagging his finger. "I had a police officer with the body at all times. He stood and watched while Hutchins cut and sliced."

"And?"

"And my man remembers clearly when Hutchins spread that poor girl's pussy open. He recalls definitely that she was wearing a blood-soaked tampon and that Hutchins remarked that only a major league weirdo would pull a girl's rag out, hide the pepperoni, then stick it back in. My man says that Hutchins never took any vaginal smears."

Ike contemplated this revelation. "You think she was raped?"

"No," said Hollister, "at least not in that apartment. We scoured the whole place for jizz—none. There's no way a man can screw a woman and not spill even a drop. If she was raped, it happened somewhere else and the perp brought her there and set the scene."

"So why didn't you go after Hutchins?"

"We did. He claimed that there was a rocket in her socket all right, but that he passed his swab around it and that my mongoloid cop never saw him do it."

"How about the report?" asked Ike. "There was no mention that Dr. Lepert was menstruating."

Hollister lit another Camel. He took several puffs, then said: "You're clever, Dr. Darnell. I didn't pick up on that fact until well after the case was closed. Anyhow, when Mrs. Lepert came up with her husband's diary, we still had nothing."

Ike asked, "But you suspect Hutchins?"

"It's hard to nail a guy with a lily white record and no firm evidence." Hollister's lips curled over his tobacco-stained dentures; they quivered. "If you come up with something, Doctor, that we can hang our hats on, you bring it to me and I'll do what I can. Frankly, I don't think you're going to find much."

Ike got up from his chair and set down his cup. "Thanks for the coffee, Captain. I'll be in touch."

Ike Darnell drove west to Auburn, replaying his conversation with Hollister over and over again. *There's too much going on here*, he thought, *to dismiss David Lepert's diary out of hand. It sure as hell appears he was absolutely right.* In a strange way he was both pleased and displeased that he had decided to withhold the existence of Marvin Hambly from Captain Hollister. *I'll find out for myself.*

Locating Alden Street, he slowed and looked for the numbers on the small frame houses. He parked in front of 124, exited, strode up the walkway and rang the bell. After a minute he rang it again. He knocked sharply on the glass panes inset in the white, metal door.

Realizing that it was 9:30 in the morning and that Hambly was probably at work and might live alone, Ike returned to the Suburban, pulled back out into traffic and stopped at a diner. He ordered black coffee and opened the Auburn Yellow Pages to the "Laboratory" section. He found five listings. He slipped into the phone booth and began dialing, asking: "May I speak with Mr. Hambly please?"

His fourth call—to Central New York Biologicals—hit paydirt. "Just a moment, sir," a lady said. Then: "Hello, this is Marvin Hambly."

"Mr. Hambly, my name is Dr. Darnell. I'd like to speak with you about Dr. Natalie Lepert. Would you have some free time today? Perhaps you could arrange to have lunch with me?"

"You from EconoMed?"

"No, I work for Mrs. Lepert, Natalie's mother. I am investigating her death."

"All right. There's a place downtown called Alfredo's. I'll see you there at 11:45. And Dr. Darnell?"

"Yes?"

"I've been waiting a hell of a long time for this day," said Marvin Hambly.

"Good. I'll see you in a couple of hours."

Ike entered Alfredo's at 11:30 and was seated at a table which gave him a clear view of the door. Just as he finished his iced tea, he spotted a man in blue overalls. A glance at his left ear confirmed his identity. Ike arose and approached the man.

"Mr. Hambly?"

"Yes?"

"I am Ike Darnell." He extended his hand, observing as he had so many times before in his life, the look of complete surprise on Marvin Hambly's countenance. *Face it, Ike,* he thought, *you sound like a goddamned honkey. When they see you're black, it scares them.*

Reluctantly, Hambly shook. Ike led him to his table. The two men studied each other. Ike noted that, despite Ardus Jenkins' artistic hands,

Hambly's left ear looked like a lump of scar tissue—not an ear. He saw a tremor of fear in Hambly's eyes.

"Please call me 'Ike.' OK if I call you 'Marvin'?"

Hambly smiled. "Sure. What did you want to talk about?"

"I'll get to that. First, I'd like to know what you meant about waiting so long for this day."

"I thought the cops'd come looking for me. I had been to Natalie's place so many times before she died, that I was sure they'd find my fingerprints—I was a GI; they definitely have my prints on file. But they didn't. No one ever contacted me about her until you did today."

"What would you have told the police if they had?" asked Ike, now first appreciating the fact that Marvin Hambly was bursting full with information he seemed compelled to get out.

"About the analyses I was doing for her."

Ike pulled out his notebook, certain that this was going to be too much even for his prehensile mind. "Marvin, please tell me what you do."

"You called me at the lab, Doc—er, Ike. You know I work there."

"But I don't know anything about that lab."

"How *did* you find me?"

"Natalie Lepert's mailman."

Hambly nodded, seemingly remembering. "The Central New York Biological Lab is the eastern regional source of purified biological extracts for Stiles Labs. Ever hear of them?"

The name struck a chord of recognition in Ike's mind, but he couldn't quite place it. He shook his head.

"It's a huge international conglomerate. They do a little of this, a little of that—all in the medical field."

"OK, Marvin. What does your lab do?"

"A lot of different things. But, me—my bag is house dust. That's why Natalie contacted me about three months before she died."

"I don't follow. House dust?"

"Yes. You're aware that allergists all over the country are giving patients shots which contain purified extracts of what they're allergic to."

Ike nodded, not having any idea what would come next.

"My job is collecting and purifying house dust and shipping it to Stiles' main plant in Dallas where it's sold in expensive little vials to the doctors who're treating all those sneezers and wheezers."

"I'm with you. So how does Natalie Lepert fit in?"

"She contacted me out of the blue one day— said she had been doing some research on the composition of Stiles' house dust extracts and had determined that Central New York Bio was the original source."

"Her research—what was she looking for?"

"She never said specifically, just that she wanted me to compare the commercially available stuff with what I collected and purified. She thought there might be a significant difference."

Ike's heart raced. "Was there?" he asked expectantly.

"It appeared that there were proteins in her samples that weren't present in mine. She paid me privately to work for her, so I had to work nights and didn't have access to the sophisticated chromatographic equipment necessary to really pin them down."

"Did she say *why* she wanted to know?"

"Not in so many words, but I think it had something to do with her father's illness. She loved her old man and would've done any—"

An overly made-up, plump waitress interrupted them. "Can I take your orders, gentlemen?"

"Veal parm with a side of spaghetti and a Coke," said Hambly.

"Same," dittoed Ike.

Ike toyed with his fork, then said: "Why did you have to go to Natalie's apartment so often?"

"She was feeding all of the data I generated into her computer. She must have had a theory about something and was recording each detail meticulously. She felt there was some magic key, some discrepancy that would explain whatever she was puzzled about. She wanted my opinion of her data." Marvin paused and stared at his tan paper placemat. "Ike, ever since I read about her in the papers, I've had this feeling that someone murdered her because of her research and I've been scared to death that they'd think I did it."

"Did you?"

"Of course not. I loved Natalie Lepert. I don't think she knew it and, well, with my disfigurement, I was sure she was not likely to feel anything for me. But still, I would've done *anything* for her. You know what I'm saying?"

Ike's heart went out to him. He knew exactly what he was saying. "What happened to Natalie's data, Marvin?"

"Don't know. If I had to guess, I'd say it was stored on her hard disk. She was a first-rate scientist, not the kind to be sloppy with her work."

Their meals arrived and they ate in silence.

Marvin set down his fork, wiped spaghetti sauce from his chin, peered into Ike's eyes and said, "I'm certain someone killed her because of that work, Ike. I don't know where she was headed or what she had discovered, but I have this sick feeling in my gut that someone at EconoMed got onto her and didn't like what he found."

Ike was startled. "EconoMed? Why EconoMed?"

"She made it clear to me that she didn't want

anyone at the clinic to know about her work. When she said that, there was fear in her eyes. She seemed terrified of somebody at the clinic."

"Did she ever mention the name 'Hutchins'?"

"Tangentially, yes. But nothing specific. Her fear spooked me, Ike. So when I learned she was dead, frankly I wasn't really surprised. I sort of knew it was coming and I think so did she."

David Lepert's diary! thought Ike Darnell.

"Tell me, Marvin—this may sound like a stupid question—but *exactly where* does your lab get the house dust you process?"

Marvin Hambly burst out laughing.

"What's so funny?"

"You're not going to believe me."

"Try me."

"We get it mostly from the Boy Scouts of America. We pay various civic groups—like the Boy Scouts—fifty cents a bag for full vacuum cleaner bags. That's how they raise funds. They send hundreds of kids into their neighborhoods to knock on doors and ask housewives if they can have their used bags. They explain to them that they can turn what would otherwise be trash into cold cash by selling it to us. They have no trouble coming up with thousands of bags every year. I get the bags, extract the proteins, purify them, then ship them to Dallas. It's as simple as that." He desultorily twirled a strand of spaghetti on his fork, then looked into Ike's eyes and asked, "Are you really a doctor?"

"Yes, Marvin. I'm a retired neurosurgeon from Philadelphia. It's a long story about how I came to be working for Mrs. Lepert." He thought, *In some bizarre and crazy way, though, I'm damned glad that I did.*

Ike told the lab tech how to get in touch with him through Sophie Lepert, should he think of anything else that he may think important, then left the restaurant and climbed into the Suburban.

On the way north several words reverberated in his mind.

Computer?
Hard disk?
Data?
House dust?
(and)

EconoMed?
A vague plan coalesced in his mind.

CHAPTER 4

1 May

Ike Darnell sat at the dining room table in Sophie Lepert's home in Ogdensburg reviewing his copious notes. Sophie entered through a tall wood-paneled swinging door from the kitchen and sat across from him. He studied her blatantly, fully aware that she watched his eyes move and consider. He saw her carefully coiffured silver-gray hair, her barely lined sharply featured face, her pale gray eyes, sensuous lips, thin frame and body and magnificently tailored blue wool suit. He watched her pour coffee into cups of fine bone china.

"Are your thoughts in order?" she asked.

Ike rested his gold Cross pen on the yellow legal pad and smiled. "Yes. But I have questions."

"Fire away."

"What happened to the contents of Natalie's apartment after her death?"

"The Syracuse police cordoned it off for five and a half months claiming that it was a crime scene in an ongoing investigation. They wouldn't let even David or me go in. They paid the rent and the utilities. Then one day we got a call saying that we had seventy-two hours to get her things out of there. We hired a local mover who brought her things back to Ogdensburg."

"Where are they?" asked Ike.

"David was very firm about that point. All of Natalie's furniture, clothes and possessions were stored in our attic here."

"Did you ever inventory it?"

"Oh, I went up a couple of times when I was feeling low. Somehow it made me feel closer to her."

"How about your husband?"

"David *never* went up there. It was too dusty. He was severely allergic to house dust and would start wheezing whenever he was exposed to a lot of it."

"So David ordered Natalie's things stored where he would never see them?"

"Yes. He was crushed by her death—it hastened his own demise; I'm sure of it."

Ike processed this information. In the midst of his thoughts he heard Sophie say: "Based upon what you've told me, Ike, I know your next question."

She went on: "You want to know whether David was being treated for his dust allergy. Yes?"

"Precisely," he said.

"For years his wheezing just wasn't that bad and he was treated by our family doctor with pills and inhalers. Then, about a year before David developed leukemia, Dr. Martin referred him to an allergist in Watertown and he was started on allergy shots."

"Did they help him?"

"Definitely. He improved within three or four months."

Ike tried desperately to put the puzzle parts together in his mind. Then: "Sophie, I believe you said that the local hospital here went HMO with EconoMed."

"That's right."

"When?"

"About five years ago."

"So this Dr. Martin works for EconoMed?"

"Yes."

"And the Watertown allergist?"

"Same. They refer only to each other except in extraordinary cases. I've never looked unfavorably on EconoMed—remember, Natalie worked for them, too."

Ike got up and began to pace. He thought of all the vicious debates he had had to referee during the last several years back in Philly when he was

President of the County Medical Society. The issue in almost all of them had been how to thwart the takeover of private practice by the dreaded HMO's. He remembered their tactics — find a handful of private docs who weren't doing so well, offer them big salaries with fringies, then approach local business and industry with the come-on that *local* doctors would be providing their employees medical care. *Some of them may not even have to change doctors!* Ike had witnessed the gradual erosion of the private health care system until, just before he had retired, the combatants were not private docs versus HMO's, but HMO A versus HMO B. He was not surprised that these changes had hit upstate New York later than the metropolitan areas.

Ike stopped his pacing in front of the huge bay window which overlooked a rose garden, twirled and said: "Sophie, do you know where Natalie's computer is?"

She nodded. "Upstairs. In the attic."

"Let's get it."

They made two trips each up to the dusty attic and reassembled the IBM PC-AT, monitor, keyboard and printer on the dining room table. Ike found an outlet, inserted the plug and switched it on.

Marvin Hambly started his car in the lab parking lot and pulled out into traffic. He had told his boss that he wasn't feeling well and got the afternoon off to recuperate. In fact, he wanted to go home so that he could call Ike Darnell in private. There was more information he thought the doctor should know.

On the way he decided to stop at the Convenience Mart three blocks from his house. He needed a quart of milk. Marvin parked outside and entered the small store.

Moments later a tan Pontiac pulled in next to Marvin's car. A man wearing a black ski mask stepped out of his vehicle, leaving the motor running. He walked slowly into the store, brandished an Uzi submachine pistol and said, "This is a stickup! Empty your register!" to the overweight teenager behind the counter.

The terrified girl complied.

The man in the ski mask turned swiftly to his right and unleashed a fusillade of bullets at the two customers standing in front of the dairy cooler. He grabbed the wad of cash from the clerk, then mowed her down with five quick rounds to the chest. He slipped the Uzi under his overcoat, left the Convenience Mart, got into the tan Pontiac and drove slowly towards the I-90 on ramp.

In thunderous silence Ike and Sophie watched the video display terminal flicker to life.

Ike was not surprised that the screen remained

completely black. He pressed several of the standard buttons he was familiar with from his own similar computer at home.

Enter – nothing.

F10 – nothing.

Ctrl/Alt/Delete simultaneously – nothing.

"What's the matter?" asked Sophie. "Didn't we hook it up properly?"

"The memory's been erased completely," said Ike glumly. "Do you know if Natalie ever made copies of her computer files for safekeeping. They would've been on small, black diskettes about the size of an old forty-five record."

"I have no idea. I've never been one to fool with computers. David would've known. He had a word processor at his law office – used to play with it all the time before he got sick."

"What happened to David's computer?"

"At his request I auctioned all of his office furniture and supplies when he went out of practice. I seem to recall that one of the local doctors bought the computer for his son in college."

"His files! Where are David's files? He practiced law for more than fifty years. What did he do with all that stuff?"

"They're all above the carriage house in neatly labeled boxes by year. Do you think he may have had any of Natalie's records?"

"I'm going to find out," said Ike Darnell, a timbre of determination in his voice.

Later, his hands and shirt smeared with dirt, Ike slumped in front of the TV set in his room at the motel in Ogdensburg. He heard the announcer report the triple murder and robbery at the Convenience Mart in Auburn, then felt as though he had been clubbed in the head when he learned that Marvin Hambly had been one of the victims.

Freshly showered and dressed, Ike was just walking into the Lepert house for dinner with Sophie when the telephone rang.

"It's for you," she said. "Tracey Barr in Syracuse — says she's returning your call."

CHAPTER 5

2 May

Dr. Harold Hutchins sat with two other men on adjacent leather chairs in the posh den of a mansion on the outskirts of Dallas, Texas.

"That was a nice piece of work, Luigi," said Stanley Schaulton, chief executive officer of EconoMed International. He was a seventy-four year old veteran businessman whose career had touched all bases—from owning professional sports teams to casinos in Vegas to huge conglomerates like EconoMed. Hutchins eyed him clinically, noting the fine tremor of his hands, the barely perceptible hesitation of his thoughts and the rigid facial musculature. *Early Parkinson's*, he thought, never aware of these defects before.

"Thanks, Mr. Schaulton," said kinky-haired Luigi Lente, an erstwhile professional kick-boxer who had worked as a "maintenance man" for Schaulton for the past nine years.

"Yep, my boy," said Schaulton, "nobody's going to read that as a hit on that Hambly fellow."

"I recommend," said Hutchins, "that we deal with Darnell more prudently. We can't just take him out."

"Why not?" asked the elderly Texan.

"I ran a trace through some confidential sources. Sophie Lepert obtained Darnell's services by virtue of an ad she placed in a national medical journal."

"So?"

"So if he goes down, there'll be another to take his place. Mrs. Lepert is extremely wealthy—her husband was heavily invested in the market and was a damned shrewd player. The old lady's got millions to play with. She could afford the best private dick. As it turns out, her decision to hire a physician was a smart one—and this Darnell is one clever guy."

"Recommendations?" asked Schaulton.

Dr. Harold Hutchins told them what he had in mind—what he had already initiated before he left Syracuse.

Ike Darnell arose before dawn, donned his sweatsuit and put in two miles of what he still referred to as "road work," a holdover from his professional boxing days. Refreshed, he returned to his motel, showered, shaved and dressed and was on the road in plenty of time to meet Tracey Barr at 11 AM in Syracuse.

Ike attempted, during the two and a half hour ride, to bring a real person into focus when he thought of Natalie Lepert. He realized that he was unable, that he simply didn't know enough about the woman herself. *Maybe that's where her girlfriend can be helpful*, he thought.

Ike was deeply bothered by the sudden death of Marvin Hambly. *Was it really a random event? Did he just happen to be in that store when it was heisted? Something isn't kosher—why would a two-bit hoodlum use a submachine gun for a three hundred dollar job?* Then, he relaxed a bit, considering himself a bit too paranoid, as he failed to see how anyone could have connected Hambly with him and his investigation. *Unless*, he thought warily, *I was followed.*

He took Tracey Barr to a swanky restaurant on Warren Street not far from the Shearson office where she worked. He found the stockbroker to be attractive, knowledgeable, diffident, articulate and full of energy. He chatted with her briefly about the business world and concluded that she'd be the kind of person he might entrust his own money to, if he weren't so damned conservative. He directed the conversation to the dead pathologist: "Tracey, I'd appreciate it if you would describe Natalie for me." He made sure that she saw the urgent look in his eyes.

"Sure. For starters, she was a brilliant girl, able to comprehend virtually anything she put her mind to—not just medicine. She was interested in art, the theatre, ballet, pro football, fly fishing—the list goes on and on. Natalie was quiet—I wouldn't say shy—just quiet. She didn't say much either to me or to anybody else, except possibly to her father whom she adored. She was compulsively neat and orderly."

"Any boyfriends?"

Tracey hesitated. "Nothing steady," she said.

Ike sensed she was hiding something. Irritated, he said, "Now come on! I've seen her pictures and some of her mother's home movies—Natalie Lepert was a very attractive woman. Why no men in her life?"

Ike watched the color drain from Tracey's face. Then: "Was she a lesbian?"

Tracey burst out laughing. "Of course not! It's just that, that . . ."

"That what? Damnit, Tracey—in all likelihood somebody murdered your friend. Do you understand what I'm saying? There probably is a live human being out there somewhere who took Natalie's life. Please don't hold back on me."

"But I promised her."

"Bad excuse. Don't you think she would want you to help find her killer?"

"All right. She was having an on-again, off-again affair for the last two years of her life."

"Who?"

"A man she worked with," said Tracey Barr softly.

"Damnit!" shrieked Ike loud enough to startle the waiter across the room. "Tell me his name!"

"His name is Harold Hutchins; he's married," she said.

"I see," replied Ike. A kaleidoscope of thoughts rushed through his mind. *Hutchins? Jesus Christ, this is starting to stink. The guy who did her autopsy was boffing her!* He wondered what Natalie Lepert's relationship with Harold Hutchins had to do with unknown proteins in house dust extract. *Is there a connection? Maybe it's a red herring? Maybe it's as straightforward as it seems: Hutchins was sleeping with her and she wanted more from him. She threatened to spill the beans to his wife and he killed her, covering it with a phony autopsy report. Unlikely. Somebody would have put it together. Somebody shrewd. Somebody like Captain Bertram Hollister.* "Tell me, Tracey—did many people know about Natalie and Hutchins?"

"No. It was extremely hush-hush because he was married."

"How did you find out?"

55

"I happened to drop by one evening and he was there. Natalie said they were discussing a patient. I didn't buy it—she was wearing a bathrobe. Later, I asked her straight out and she told me. I promised never to breathe a word of it to anyone."

"Did the police speak to you after her death?" asked Ike.

"Yes. They asked me the same question you did and I lied to them."

Ike looked at her fiercely.

"They said she died naturally or killed herself, Dr. Darnell. I didn't want to sully her name."

"Do you think she killed herself, Tracey?"

"It's possible. She was extremely upset about her Dad. She made trips all over the country researching his illness."

Ike was shocked. Sophie had mentioned nothing to him about any trips. "Trips? Where? When?"

"I didn't go with her; she just happened to mention them. She took long weekends to speak with other pathologists and to show them Mr. Lepert's blood slides. She said that no one had been able to establish a diagnosis at EconoMed and that he was considered untreatable. Natalie even sent him to the Lahey Clinic—they gave her the same report."

Ike chewed on his sirloin, even more puzzled than when he had sat down with Tracey Barr. He saw her look at her watch. "I'm afraid I've got to get back to my desk, Dr. Darnell. If there's anything else I can help you with, call me again." She got up from the table.

"Tracey, did Natalie ever make copies of her computer's memory onto diskette?"

"Of course. Every night. She kept the diskettes in a fireproof box in her desk. She said you never knew, that you couldn't be too careful. Bye, Doctor. Thank you for lunch."

Ike ate two scoops of vanilla ice cream slowly, mulling over his next moves between spoonfuls.

He paid the check and left the restaurant. Deciding to leave his car in the Shearson underground garage, he hailed a cab.

"Where to, brother?" asked the elderly black man behind the wheel.

"EconoMed Clinic," he replied.

Ike walked into the main lobby from street level and approached the reception desk. He saw that the sultry blond had been replaced by a stunning light-skinned black woman who appeared to be in her early forties. He marveled at her girlish figure, her thick sensual lips and her aura of control and energy. He waited behind a dumpy old lady who asked, between coughs, for directions to the X-ray Department, then said, "Excuse me, ma'am. Would you ring Dr. Hutchins' office for me? Please tell him that Dr. Darnell would like to see him."

The black lady checked a roster on the desk

before her. "I am sorry, Doctor, but Dr. Hutchins is not in today. Could someone else help you?"

Her smile! Ike's knees were jelly. "No," he managed, "Do you know when he'll be back?"

She glanced down. "According to my list, he should be in tomorrow morning. Care to leave a message?"

Ike shook his head. He stared at her smile, realizing that the perfect teeth were real. "No, thank you. I'd appreciate it, though, if you'd call me a cab."

The receptionist looked at her watch. "I'm going off duty right now. May I give you a lift?"

Ike's smile was total. "That would be mighty nice of you, ma'am."

"My name's Dahlia; Dahlia Lennox." She extended her lovely hand.

"Ike; Ike Darnell."

Dahlia snatched up her purse and left the reception area. "Where are you headed, Ike?"

"Syracuse Police Department. Will that take you out of your way?"

"No. I'm going right by there."

They took the exit from the lobby marked "PARKING GARAGE."

"So what do you think, Captain?" asked Ike after telling Hollister all that he had learned about Natalie Lepert, including the Marvin Hambly liaison.

"I think you're onto something, Doctor, but I'm not sure what." He paused and lighted a Camel. "Why the fuck didn't you tell me about this Hambly character?"

Ike was uneasy. "I didn't know if it would pan out. I figured I'd check him out first. I had no idea he was going to be killed the next day. By the way, do you know if the police down in Auburn have come up with anything on the murderer?"

"Yeh," responded the detective, "they notified us of everything they had." He held up his left hand, making an "O" with his thumb and index finger. "We've never seen that MO before. I don't know how things are in Philly, but in central New York punks don't carry Uzis."

Ike sipped at his coffee. "Any suggestions?"

Hollister blew a series of concentric smoke rings. "Keep doing what you're doing, Doctor. You've come up with more in a few days than we did in months. Obviously, the key here will be to get at and break Hutchins."

"You think he killed her?"

"Not sure; but I'd bet my asshole he knows a hell of a lot more than he's letting on. Just get me something I can sink my teeth into and I'll take this case back to the D.A. I need something hard, something real, something documentable—not fucking suspicions."

Ike nodded.

"Say, Doctor, I'm heading out for a bite. Care to join me?"

"Another time, Captain. I've got some plans for tonight."

Ike found Dahlia Lennox's town house in Baldwinsville without difficulty. At her gracious offer he broke down and drank two ounces of scotch. He truly enjoyed the ambience, the chance to let his hair down and say silly things to a beautiful woman.

Gallantly, he took her arm and led her to the Suburban.

"My, my, Ike! A rich doctor like you driving a Chevy truck."

"I got sick of Mercedeses and Audis—you could never get them serviced. This hulk always starts and has never broken down." He opened the door for her and helped her in. On the way around to the driver's seat he experienced his first pangs of guilt. *Marilyn, please forgive me, but it's been real hard being alone all this time. I know you understand, honey—don't you?*

They dined at La Boheme, enjoying the fine food and the roving violinist.

Over aperitifs Dahlia asked, "Why don't you tell me more about this forensic investigation you're working on? Is it a malpractice case?"

"I don't mean to be rude, but I'm afraid that I

have to respect patient confidentiality," he lied. "Maybe once everything's out in the open, I might be able to discuss it. Say, I've been meaning to ask you: how long you been working at the clinic. I was there just the other day at about the same time and there was a foxy white girl at your desk."

She chuckled, low, throaty and tumescently sexy. "Oh, *her*. She's just gone on vacation and I'm filling in for the next two weeks. I usually work in administration."

Ike sipped his liqueur. "Where are you from? Originally, I mean."

"L.A."

"And how did a lovely lady like you get transplanted from sunny California to a place like Syracuse?"

"About a year before my husband died, he was transferred here. He was an executive with Carrier Corporation. I stayed on."

Later, in bed, his eyes wide open, his fingertips gently stroking the velvety skin of her back and buttocks, Ike felt more like a real human being than he had since his tragedy.

Before dawn he dressed. At the doorway he kissed her chastely on the forehead while passing the balls of his thumbs over the erect nipples which poked through her flimsy peignoir.

"Call me soon, Ike. Please?"

"He kissed her again, parting her lips with his tongue. "Count on it," he said.

Once in the Suburban heading north towards Ogdensburg, Ike decided that a detailed search of Natalie Lepert's belongings in the attic would be next on his agenda. He was mentally creating a schedule for the day, when he noticed the flashing red and blue lights rapidly approaching the Suburban from the rear.

He pulled over to the shoulder and got out.

"What's the prob—" he began.

The tall thin State Trooper interrupted: "OK, fella, hands against the truck and spread em. No funny stuff."

Shocked, Ike complied, peering curiously over his shoulder while the second trooper searched his truck.

"Well, well, WELL!" he heard the man say. "Now lookey what we have here!"

"What is it, Chris?" asked the cop immediately behind Ike.

"Nose candy. Feels like about fifteen keys—and a satchel full of cash." He approached Ike with a bounce in his step. "You know, champ, that you're in very deep shit. Very."

The first Trooper said, "You are under arrest. You have the right to remain silent. Anything you say can and will . . ."

CHAPTER 6

2 May

Thoroughly alone, a shattered man, Ike Darnell sat in the corner of his cell thinking how much the way he felt now was like the way he felt in the fifth round of the Buddy DeVita fight.

It was the summer after his freshman year at Yale. The old arena in Norristown. Cheering throngs of blacks and whites filled the stands. He'd had his way with DeVita, a monstrous Italian from Pittsburgh, during the first four rounds, administering an effective paint job with snapping jabs, sharp left hooks and several crushing overhand rights. Then ten seconds into the fifth DeVita feinted with a lead right, flicked out a lazy left, bent his knees, crouched and delivered a brutal right uppercut to Ike's jaw. Up at the count of six, his vision blurred, Ike moved woodenly trying to fend off DeVita's thunderous assault. He found himself pinned in the corner, experiencing power, pain and humiliation—much as he was right now in this obscenely small jail cell—until mercifully the ref had stopped the fight.

Ike thought, *That was the toughest hundred bucks I ever earned.* He had had to box to put himself through school. Ike's father owned a shoe repair shop adjacent to their West Philadelphia home. The Darnell family wasn't dirt poor, but college tuition was out of the question. With his fight money and a meager academic scholarship, he did ultimately make it. *And now*, he thought, *I've been booked, arraigned and thrown into the clink like a common criminal. I should have listened to my Daddy: "Ike, remember one thing—always keep your pecker in your pants."*

The clanging of metal against metal interrupted his reverie. Ike looked up and saw that someone was entering his cell.

"I want to hear your story once more, Doctor," said Detective Captain Bertram Hollister who sat on a wooden chair opposite Ike.

Though dejected and very tired, Ike mustered the mental energy to go over again with Hollister every detail of his encounter with Dahlia Lennox. He finished with: "Did you check her town house?"

"Sure did. Empty. Super says it hasn't been occupied in four months."

"WHAT? Just last night it was completely furnished—pictures of her husband on the wall, full refrigerator, towels in the bathroom—the whole bit."

"I went there myself. It was completely empty. However, Ike—I may call you Ike?—I believe your story."

"Why? Why do you believe me?"

"The perfume in the air—it was fresh and it matched the odor on your clothes. Further, no matter how well they—whoever *they* are—tried to clean that place, there's no way they could get everything. Dollars to doughnuts we find your hairs and fibers from your clothing on the carpet."

"So I can get out of here?"

"Yes. But not on that score—it's just circumstantial. Remember legally you're being held for possession of one fuck of a lot of cocaine. In New York State that's a very big deal. You'll be sprung within the hour because Mrs. Lepert put up the hundred grand bail. She got you a shrewd Jewish lawyer, too—a slick by the name of Arnie Weinstein. They don't come any better. You're lucky."

Ike sighed. "How about EconoMed? Did they give you any info on their black receptionist?"

"Yes, according to them, they never had any black receptionist. Their girl's a blond—and a real looker."

Suddenly, Ike pictured the old woman with the

cough who had asked directions to X-ray. He told Hollister about her. The detective said he would check.

Ike Darnell parked his Suburban in front of Sophie Lepert's house just at noon. Before he was out of the vehicle he saw Sophie rushing down the front steps to greet him. She hugged his massive frame, both laughing and crying. "You big oaf!" she said finally. Slapping her knees she gave in to the absurdity in her mind; laughter poured out of her. "Cocaine and a hooker—Ike, you *do* have *chutzpah*!"

He led her inside and they sat in the front parlor. He told her everything he had learned from Tracey Barr and about the Dahlia Lennox caper, while snacking on coffee and doughnuts.

"So what's next?" asked Sophie.

"I've got to go through Natalie's belongings with a fine tooth comb. First, I must find her receipts for air fare, hotels and so on for six months to a year before she died. Second, if possible, I must determine the whereabouts of her fireproof box—do you remember ever seeing it?"

"No."

Ike passed his maw of a hand across the stubble on his chin. "I see. And third, I've got to try to get a make on this Dahlia Lennox."

"Certainly that's not her real name?"

"True, but the more I think about her, the more I realize that she was too beautiful a woman to be a total unknown."

Sophie was puzzled. "I don't follow."

"My gut feeling is that she is, or was, an actress or a model or the like. Hence, there must be publicity photos of her somewhere in this country."

"It's a big country."

"Yes, but I have a close friend in Atlantic City, Alonzo Peets—one of the slickest black bucks you'd ever want to meet. He wears many hats. Amongst other things he's been an agent for black female talent of all sorts for the past twenty years. If I'm ever going to beat this phony cocaine rap, I've got to go to Atlantic City and pore through his picture books. Five'll get you ten he's got a snap of the woman who set me up. It's a long shot, but I've got to try. I don't fancy doing fifteen big ones in Dannemora."

Together they climbed the stairs and entered the attic. Sophie led Ike to the several cartons of her daughter's papers. He found without difficulty the one marked "FINANCIAL" for the year of Natalie's death.

Opening the box Ike had the feeling that beneath his dirty fingertips there lay an answer—in what form he could not guess—to the question of why Natalie Lepert died. He sifted through the receipts pulling out obvious credit card monthly statements and placed them in a pile without examining them first. He saw that Sophie was rooting through other piles in search of the fireproof box. He picked up the first, a VISA bill from the month of February, scanned it, but noted nothing of apparent significance. Then March. Then April.

"Sophie!" he shouted. She moved to his side.

"Look at these." Ike held up statements for May, June, July and August. She took them.

Then, after a full minute, she said, "Ike, I see what you mean. Natalie must have stayed at this hotel—the Yankee Carriage House in New Haven, Connecticut—four or five times."

"Six. She used her VISA to pay them six times from, uh, May fifth through August twelfth—"

"—a week before she died!"

Ike nodded. "And each visit lasted for two or three days. She went just about every two weeks. And look at this—on the August statement is written: 'PAID, #3452' in a different handwriting from the rest."

Sophie examined the paper. "That's David's writing. Despite his mental deficiencies, he insisted on handling her estate."

"I see," said Ike. "Did he ever comment on Natalie's trips? Do you think he knew about them?"

"I don't know. He never mentioned anything."

Ike thought silently for several long seconds. "Sophie, I'm going to go downstairs and call my friend in Atlantic City. I'll tell him everything I know about that woman and I'll ask him to get back to you here. If he comes up with something, get in touch with me immediately. Meanwhile, you keep looking for the fireproof box. I shouldn't be gone for more than a few days."

"Gone? Where?"

"New Haven. I've got to find out why Natalie went there and whom she was meeting."

"Ike, the terms of your bail make it necessary for you to stay in New York State."

"I should be back before anyone knows."

"And if you're not?"

"Then I'm not."

Ninety minutes later, the back of his Suburban packed with clothes and a new briefcase of cash, Ike drove south and east. He was too engrossed in his thoughts and too much of an amateur to notice the tan Pontiac which followed the same route as he.

CHAPTER 7

3 May

Ike Darnell awakened at first light. He had
been tired from the long drive when he checked in
late last night to the Yankee Carriage House on
Whitney Avenue in New Haven. He had asked no
questions — simply took his room key and headed
for bed. Now, eager to get up, get moving and find
some answers, Ike sprang out of bed, stripped off
his pajamas, urinated, then donned his sweatsuit,
pocketed his key and left the small room.

As he ran through the early morning haze, he
experienced an extraordinary high, a rush — for he
had jogged through these same streets thirty-five
years before. He felt that he had somehow come
full circle, that for some unfathomable reason, fate
had brought him back to Mother Yale. His muscu-
lar legs bounded over curbs and onto dew-wet
cement. He passed by the buildings where he had

studied and learned and matured—where he had endured open prejudice to become a scholar and a man. *There was no Marilyn then*, he thought. It was before the long grueling days and nights of hospital duty, brilliant lights in operating theaters, patients dying in his arms, survivors smiling, grateful for his expert care. *They were idyllic times, times of youth—my rite of passage. And then, in a flash, there was my career. So fast, it seemed. The years—they seemed like seconds, like minutes.* He crossed an empty street, his mind open, thinking of the day that Vinny Parisi had first consulted him about his horrible back pain, the operation to repair his herniated disk, the disgruntlement that followed, the threatening letters and calls. *Why didn't I take them seriously? Why didn't I appreciate that Parisi was a whacko, that he was likely to do what he said he would do? I chose to ignore him. He destroyed my life—and I am to blame. I shall feel that guilt until my dying day, knowing that I killed my family, just as if I had pulled the trigger.* Every six clops of his running shoes rekindled the image of the bloodbath at the Bellevue-Stratford. His mind racing, his heart pounding, his pain overwhelming, Ike Darnell returned to the hotel not having thought at all about Natalie Lepert's bloated, pungent body lying naked in her bed or of the beautiful black woman who had conned him, had made him a criminal in the eyes of the law.

Ike showered and dressed. He consumed a huge

breakfast, then walked with determination, his jaw set, to the office of the Yankee Carriage House. He would find out what he wanted so desperately to know.

Ike entered the well-lit room, his eyes focusing immediately on the dark-haired, ferret-faced man whose body seemed firmly rooted to the red Formica counter by two thin elbows. Ike walked up to the counter. "Excuse me, sir?"

He watched the man slowly lower his racing tabloid, then heard him say, "What can I do for you, skipper?"

Ike extracted the photograph of Natalie Lepert from his pocket and laid it on the counter. "Have you ever seen this woman?"

The ferret eyes sprang downwards, then up, like ping-pong balls. "You a cop?"

"No. Private investigator." *Why not let it all hang out?* Ike thought. *That's the kind of stuff they say on television.*

The dark-haired man smiled broadly, revealing heavily stained, gapped teeth. "Well, Mister Private Eye, I just been diagnosed as having an unusual form of Alzheimer's and I don't remember so well." He raised his eyebrows and pursed his lips.

"Sorry to hear that. How's it odd?"

"S'got a weird cure."

Ike nodded. "Go on."

"It's real funny. My brain don't work so good.

73

Then, just by looking at pictures of U.S. presidents—Presto! I got total recall. They're writing me up in a journal; my doc says it's amazing."

Ike pulled out his wallet and removed a crisp note. "Sorry, my friend. All I've got is Ben Franklin's picture. He was never president. Too bad." He held up the hundred.

The proprietor snatched it from Ike. "He'll do," he said. Then, studying the snapshot, he added, "She stayed here maybe a half dozen times. Two, three years ago. Always on weekends. Quiet. Minded her own business. Carried a briefcase." Swiftly, he picked up his racing sheet and turned a page.

"Did she ever have any visitors?" asked Ike. Now aware of the rules of the game, he raised a fifty to eye level.

"U.S. Grant," said the man. "Damned fine president." He picked the bill out of the air with a snap. Staring at the photo again, he said, "Yeh, as a matter of fact she did. Same guy every time. He'd come in here and ask me to ring her room. Then they'd go into the restaurant or to her room. Never saw him leave."

"Describe him."

"Tall. Thin. Bald. Gray hair. Bout fifty, fifty-five. Smoked a pipe. Well-dressed."

Ike placed another fifty on top of the tabloid. "Keep going," he commanded.

"He had one of those stethoscopes sticking out of his pocket—had to have been a doctor." The man snapped his fingers. "And oh yeah! Almost forgot; there's something else you should know. He had one of those—" Suddenly the man's eyes went blank, his face slack. "The cure's wearing off," he said solemnly.

Another hundred had a remarkable effect.

"You know that thing that that Russkie, Garbagechev—whatever his name was—had on his forehead?"

"A birthmark?"

"Yep. He had one of those on his left cheek. Bright red. Looked kind of swollen. Bout the size of a silver dollar and shaped like a maple leaf. Not the kind of guy you'd forget, assuming you had a good mind."

Ike removed a wad of bills from his wallet. "Anything else, my friend?"

The man's eyes bulged. He stroked his chin. "Now that you ask, yeh. He drove a silver Mercedes, always left it right out front."

Ike allowed another bill to drift from his hand, turned and left.

Ike parked the Suburban on tree-lined St. Ronan Street, in the very shadow of Yale's Science Complex, then entered the red brick building of the Connecticut State Medical Society. He'd been here years ago during his residency for the mandatory interview necessary to obtain his medical license. He found the lobby the same as he remembered it—poorly lit, elegant in a stuffy sort of way and smelling of must. Ike strode to the receptionist's desk.

"Good morning, sir. May I help you?" asked the wizened little lady with blue hair.

"I am Dr. Darnell. Is Dr. Easton still here?"

"No, Doctor. He retired five years ago. Dr. Emelius is our new Executive Director."

"May I have a moment of his time?"

"Are you a member of the Society?"

"I used to be," said Ike.

She lifted her phone, engaged in a brief conversation, then said, "Second door on your left."

Ike knocked once, heard "ENTER!" screamed, then went in. He crossed three yards of plush carpet and extended his hand. "Dr. Emelius, I am Dr. Isaac Darnell. I was a member of your society a few years back before I moved to Pennsylvania."

"Pleased to meet you, Doctor. Have a chair."

As he sat, Ike saw Emelius punch the keyboard of the computer terminal on his desk. Emelius appeared to be about Ike's age. He was a small, compact, lithe man whose sparse gray hair poorly hid the wide, raised, angry-looking scar on the left side of his scalp. *Recent craniotomy*, thought Ike, who had performed many such operations. *Must have had a brain tumor removed or had an aneurysm clipped—probably forced him to retire and take this desk job.*

"I'm sorry, Doctor," Ike heard Emelius saying, "but I must ask you some basic questions. As you know, a lot of folks claim to be people they're not for a variety of reasons."

"Certainly. I understand." Ike was well aware that physician impostors were not rare, that men like Emelius were smart to be careful. "You need to check my identity. What do you want to know?" he said, mindful that precious few blacks had been members of the prestigious Connecticut Society when he was.

Emelius stared at his terminal. "Your father's middle name?"

"Artis."

"Your mother's maiden name?"

"Tyson."

"Your chief surgeon's nickname?"

"Butcher Boy," replied Ike with a smile, recalling the invariably blood-stained white smock Dr. William Blynn always wore.

Adolph Emelius pressed the F10 button and exited from Ike's file. He stood and proffered his hand again. "Had to check, Ike." They shook. "My friends call me Dolph. How may I help you?"

"No need to make excuses. I am looking for a

man who I believe to be a local physician. I can describe him, but don't know his name."

Emelius lighted a briar pipe. Ike saw that his right hand was tremulous. Emelius puffed vigorously, raising a cloud of bluish, fragrant smoke. "Why?" he asked laconically.

Ike recounted the essentials of Natalie Lepert's death, his own investigative role, her trips to New Haven and the motel proprietor's representation of her visitor. He was puzzled at Adolph Emelius' reaction, not sure why his teal eyes narrowed and his forehead wrinkled.

"Ike, you have just drawn me a picture of Dr. Peter Tillers, former Chief of Allergy and Immunology at Yale-New Haven Hospital."

Excited, Ike asked, "Where can I find him?"

His expression grim, Emelius said, "In the Grove Street Cemetery."

"He's dead?"

Emelius nodded.

"When?"

"When did your Dr. Lepert die?"

"Mid-August, three years ago."

"About a month later. He was shot down in cold blood by a mugger outside his apartment. A brilliant man killed for sixty bucks—a tragedy.

Immediately, Ike was suspicious. Could it be a coincidence? Possibly. "Was Tillers straight clinical or was he a lab man, too?"

"Both. Besides his huge allergy practice, he conducted extensive research on the molecular structures of allergenic proteins. Tillers was world class. His lab was in the old Sterling Hall of Medicine. Perhaps Dr. Lepert was consulting him regarding his area of expertise. I suggest you see Dr. Frymoyer, the new chief."

"Thanks, Dolph. I am grateful for your assistance." Ike left without letting on that Adolph Emelius' neurosurgery scars were so obvious.

Thirty-five minutes later Ike sat across the desk from Dr. J.D. Frymoyer, his jaw agape. He'd had no clue from the sign above the door that J.D. stood for Judith Danielle and that Yale's new allergy chief was a good-looker, exceptionally polished and black. He gave her a thumbnail sketch of the reason why he was inquiring about Dr. Peter Tillers, including the fact that Natalie Lepert had suspected the presence of unusual proteins in Central New York Biological's house dust extracts.

Frymoyer listened without interrupting. Gazing pointedly into Ike's eyes, she said, "If I understand you correctly, Doctor, you believe that Dr. Lepert was murdered and that it may have had something to do with the house dust. Further, that Pete Tillers was helping her analyze that extract. Am I correct?"

"That's my belief," said Ike, captivated by her sculpted features, perfect teeth, sensuous lips and shapely figure—at least what he could see of it beneath her lab coat. "What has become of Dr. Tillers' research notes?" he asked.

"I have them. We are continuing his extraordinary work."

"Do you recall any mention of the name, Lepert, or of any house dust experiments?"

"Not off the top of my head, but I shall check for you promptly. You see, Dr. Darnell, I have never believed that Peter's murder was the random act of a mugger after some fast cash."

"No?"

"No. His killer *did* take a small amount of cash from Peter's wallet, but he left a three thousand dollar, diamond-studded Rolex on his wrist and three gold rings, laden with precious gems, on his fingers. I made my suspicions known to the New Haven Police, but they let it drop, telling me that the mugger just didn't see those items. It doesn't wash, does it?"

"No," said Ike.

"Where are you staying, Doctor? I'll find out what I can and get back to you."

"I'd appreciate it, Dr. Frymoyer. I hope to talk to you soon." He gave her the information, then left.

Back in his room, Ike made extensive mental notes of the facts he'd garnered, while waiting for

Sophie Lepert to answer her phone in Ogdensburg.

"Hello."

"Sophie, it's Ike. Any word from Mr. Peets in Atlantic City?"

"Yes. He called about an hour ago." She gave him the number. "He said he's got what he thinks you need. Ike, what's going on? Why did Natalie go to New Haven?"

"There was a doctor here at Yale, an immunologist, who was probably working on that protein Natalie thought was unusual. He was killed about a month after Natalie. I don't think it was a coincidence. Right now I'm trying to determine exactly what he was doing. Does the name, Peter Tillers, mean anything to you?"

"No."

"I'll get back to you as soon as I can. And please call me—leave a message, if necessary—if Captain Hollister is looking for me. Bye."

Thirty seconds later Ike heard the rich, earthy euphemisms of Alonzo Peets: "You, ma man, am in some real deep shit. How you git your ass conned like that?"

"It happened, Lonnie. That's all I can say. I'm not used to dealing with dirtballs. What do you have for me?"

"OK, you think that that black-assed pussy a yours was about forty or so?"

"About."

"I got PR photos of every black girl between thirty-five and fifty in the country who's been a contestant in a beauty pageant, done any actin or any modelin. If you're right about the ultra-high quality of this cooze, then she's in there. You point her out, ma friend, and I'll find her for you. Now where do I send em?"

Ike gave him the name and address of his hotel, instructed him to send the package Federal Express, thanked him, and hung up.

Luigi Lente entered the phone booth on the corner directly opposite the Yankee Carriage House. Keeping the blue Suburban in view he inserted quarters and dialed.

"Yes?" said Stanley Schaulton in Dallas.

"It's me. Our big dude is getting too damned close."

"Explain."

Luigi told him about Ike's itinerary for the day.

"I see," said Schaulton pensively. "I don't give a crap what that candy-ass Hutchins thinks. Take him out, Luigi, and make it look like an accident if you can."

"When?"

"Now."

"You got it."

Ike parked the Suburban and walked across the neatly manicured lot with boyish exuberance. When Dr. Frymoyer had called, she had said, "Hello, Dr. Darnell, this is Judy Frymoyer," to which he had responded, "Hi, Judy. Please call me Ike." Now, as he entered the vestibule of her apartment building in the center of New Haven, he had very positive feelings about both the woman and what she had to tell him. He stepped off the elevator at the sixteenth floor penthouse, saw the single oak door and rang the bell. Ike looked at his watch and saw that it was eight-thirty PM.

The elegance of the penthouse apartment matched that of Judy Frymoyer, who led Ike through an all white, dimly lit foyer into an expansive, glassed-in living room with an astounding view of New Haven, from Harkness Tower to Long Island Sound to the spires of Yale-New Haven Hospital. Spread out on a massive crystal table Ike saw several bound ledgers and two piles of computer printouts.

Judy Frymoyer switched on the overhead light. "Drink?" she asked.

"Thank you. Scotch, if you have it."

Judy fixed the drinks then brought them in on a silver tray with a plate of canapes. Placing it down and sitting across from Ike, she said, "Ike, Peter Tillers was doing some work for Natalie Lepert. Open the ledger marked 'G-2' to page 134."

Ike looked at the ultra-neat, almost calligraphic writing at the top of the page: *16 June—results of PG separation experiments, third protocol (source of assay sample: David Lepert-E).* The rest of the sheet was covered with neat columns of numbers, as were the next six pages. Ike leafed through the remainder of the book. Every five or ten pages there were brief annotations regarding PG ratios, solubility indices, bioassay purities and antigenicity. Ike looked at Judy. "What does it mean?"

She sipped her vodka and tonic. "I've been through it all—that's twice now. The first time I reviewed Peter's notes, shortly after his death, I focused on the work I had been familiar with. You know, the stuff we'd talk about over lunch and at conferences. He'd never mentioned this PG stuff and it meant nothing to me. That, of and by itself, I find odd, as Peter and I had a very good working relationship."

"What's PG?" asked Ike, not wishing to appear an imbecile, but having no idea. Absently, he plucked a miniature bronze Remington statue from the end table and ran his fingers over its surface.

"I don't know," she said softly. "It could stand for 'prostaglandin.' It appears that Peter was devoting virtually all of his time to its study from May through September of that year."

"That, of course, coincides precisely with Natalie Lepert's weekend visits to New—"

Ike heard the doorbell ring.

Judy walked swiftly through the foyer and peered through the peephole. "Yes?"

Ike listened to Judy's side of the conversation, gripping the Remington bust nervously, then saw the door open and the New Haven Police Officer enter the apartment. He heard Judy say, "He's right here, Officer," then, "Ike, you should thank this man. He caught two kids breaking in to your truck."

The thin, kinky-haired man appeared under the arch between the foyer and the living room. Ike observed the cold professionalism in his eyes before he spied the drawn .44 Magnum pistol.

Judy Frymoyer crossed behind the policeman coming to his side, a smile on her face. Judy said, "Ike, he stopped them before they actu—"

Luigi Lente grabbed Judy by the arm, jamming the barrel of the gun into her ribs. "OK, Darnell," he said in a frosty voice, "stand up and open the balcony doors. No fast moves or I put a hole in the lady's chest. MOVE!"

Ike arose slowly and stared at the silencer tip of the gun, realizing that no one would hear the shot. In measured tones he said, as he approached the glass doors, "Why don't you just shoot us both, hot-shot? Why fool around on the balcony?" He sensed somehow that whoever sent this slug was trying to make his death appear accidental. *Like*

Natalie's. He placed his left hand on the brass lever of the door. In his right he still grasped firmly the bronze statue.

"Move it, asshole, or I'm gonna drill this babe."

Ike pocketed the Remington and opened the french door. He stepped out onto the balcony and peered down, seeing several cars parked in front of the entrance to the building. Ike looked into the kinky-haired man's eyes. He said, "You picked a bad spot, my friend, to throw us over. We're right over the entrance—must be a dozen people down there. How would you ever get out?"

Ike saw that the man in the blue coat was considering these words carefully.

"OK," said Lente, "let's go; we're going for a ride. And don't forget—one fast move and she's a goner." He jammed the pistol into Judy's chest forcefully for effect.

Luigi Lente led Ike and Judy down the rear fire stairs, not letting go of the terrified woman for an instant. They exited at the rear of the building on a delivery ramp. "This way," said Lente, pointing.

When they reached the tan Pontiac Lente said to Ike, "You drive. I'll be sitting in the back seat with your friend." He opened the rear door, pushed Judy in and slid next to her.

For an instant Ike knew that he could have run, but that he would have sacrificed Judy Frymoyer.

He put the thought out of mind and slipped behind the steering wheel.

Lente gave him specific directions, making it clear to Ike that the gunman had worked out an alternative plan to forcing them off the balcony. Ike found himself driving out Whitney Avenue, right by the Yankee Carriage House towards Hamden. "Whom do you work for, friend?" asked Ike.

After a silence Lente said, "A very important man."

"I see," said Ike. "Why does this man want to kill me?" There was no question in his mind what the gunman intended to do.

"You been snooping where you shouldn'ta been."

"Natalie Lepert?"

"Keep driving, fartbreath. Turn right at the next light."

Ike realized that he was entering East Rock Park and was climbing to the precipice which overlooked eastern New Haven. He had come here many times to study during his student days. On sunny Saturdays and Sundays. But never at night. Reaching the summit Ike heard the man order him to stop the car. He did and, for the first time, he realized that Judy Frymoyer had lost consciousness and was slumped over on the rear seat. *No wonder she hasn't said anything,* he thought. He switched off the ignition.

Leaving the unconscious woman Lente opened his door. He moved the pistol, placing the barrel against Ike's neck. "OUT!" he said.

As Ike walked slowly towards the drop-off he reasoned, *He's not going to shoot me. It's supposed to look like an accident. He's going to push me off, then throw Judy over after.* Absently, his hand went into his pocket and grasped the bronze Remington.

"Stop," he heard. Ike felt the cold tip of the silencer against his right ear.

"OK, lover boy, put these in your pocket." He reached his left hand in front of Ike's face.

Ike grasped the object dangling from the gun-man's fingertips, felt it, was puzzled. He heard the man say, "Rubbers, numb nuts. The cops'll find you and that bitch down there smashed to shit. They'll come up with the rubbers and will put two and two together. A coupla hot-blooded folks in heat. Lost their footing—boom! A fuckin tragedy."

Ike fingered the bronze statue. "Tell me one thing first."

"What?"

"The man you work for. His name and why he gives a damn about who killed Natalie Lepert."

Ike felt the man's left hand make contact with his left shoulder blade. He moved his foot. Pebbles rolled off the edge. Many seconds later he heard tiny pings. He heard the man say, "His name's

Stanley Schaulton. It all has to do with allergy shots."

Ike knew that the thrust was coming any second. "Allergy shots?" With his right hand he lobbed the Remington laterally.

It landed with a loud, metallic *thwock*.

Lente turned reflexively towards the sound.

Ike drove his right elbow full force into the gunman's right chest. He twirled on the ball of his right foot, went into a crouch and came up with a vicious left hook, aiming it where he thought the man's head would be.

Ike knew from the sound and the feel of the blow that he had broken the man's nose. He heard the gun drop to the soft dirt, then stepped forward away from the ledge, expecting to make contact with the man. His step was unimpeded.

Where is the bastard? Ike thought just before a brutal kick struck his Adam's apple. He went down, saw flashing lights, felt a bizarre, hollow reverberation inside his head. He looked up through dazed eyes, thinking it was the Buddy DeVita fight all over again. He sensed another blow coming from the darkness.

He ducked.

Ike reached out into the black space before him, his hand finding purchase on the gunman's cloth coat. Savagely, he pulled the off-balance man towards him, drilling his midsection with a fierce straight left. Ike followed with a right uppercut, catching the point of the man's chin. He heard a sickening snap.

He lost control.

He was back in Norristown. It was round five, but now, magically, he was *winning*, he was pounding Buddy DeVita to a bloody pulp.

Still holding the erstwhile gunman, Ike rose to his feet. He delivered a right cross. A left jab. Another right. Now the man he believed to be Vinny Parisi slumped to the ground. He kicked what he thought was the man's neck, heard an unknown liquid spill and drip. Ike dropped to his knees, hammering the face with his massive fists again and again.

The Pontiac's headlights snapped on, freezing the image of Ike Darnell, his truculent face distorted by hatred and whipped by adrenalin, his left fist raised high in the air, his right hand clenching a blue uniform out of which protruded a distorted, bloodied lump of flesh and kinky, black hair.

"Stop, Ike! STOP!" shrieked Judy Frymoyer. She rushed to him and buried her head in his chest. Ike let go of the man, then, in a bizarre transition from pugilist to physician, he reached down and felt for a pulse.

Judy's tear-clouded eyes were wide. "Is he dead?"

"Yes," said Dr. Isaac Darnell. "Very. Are you OK?"

Judy pulled back from him and patted her face, chest and abdomen with the palms of her hands. She nodded. She looked at Ike more carefully. "You're bleeding. Are you all right?"

"I've been hit harder," he said.

CHAPTER 8

4 May

Detective Captain Bertram Hollister thanked the forensic man on the other end of the phone, then dialed Ike Darnell's motel room in Ogdensburg. Not finding him in and anxious to reveal what he'd just learned, Hollister called Sophie Lepert. She answered on the third ring. "Hello?"

"Mrs. Lepert, this is Captain Hollister. Can you tell me where I can reach Dr. Darnell?"

"He's out fishing. I expect him later."

"Please tell him to call me promptly."

"Of course," she said, just before hanging up and tapping out the number of the Yankee Carriage House in New Haven, Connecticut.

Ike's first realization upon awakening was that Judy had gone. He remembered the events of last night—his kidnaping, his near-death, his killing the man with his bare hands, then leaving the body and the car in the darkness and walking with Judy back to his room. He recalled her tender ministrations to his wounds, her soft caresses, then — then what? Nothing came to mind.

Ike squinted through swollen eyes and saw bright sunshine pelting his window, realizing that it was midmorning. He got to his feet and was headed for the bathroom when he heard the knock on the door.

Suddenly thrust back into the mind-frame of last night's maelstrom, Ike paused, holding his breath.

There was another knock, a louder one.

Ike spotted the silencer-equipped pistol on the end table, only now remembering that he had taken it. Holding the gun under his bathrobe, he opened the door.

A man in a gray uniform said, "Dr. Isaac Darnell?"

"Yes?"

"Package. Ya gotta sign here."

Balancing the heavy firearm with his left arm, Ike scribbled his signature, thanked the Federal Express man and took the package sent by Alonzo Peets. He sat on the edge of the bed and opened it.

Ike studied the top photograph of a gorgeous, naked black woman and saw that at its bottom, neatly typed, was a name, address and telephone number. He estimated that he was holding four or five hundred such pictures.

Stridently, the phone rang.

Setting the pile down on the floor, Ike answered, hoping that it was Judy Frymoyer, "Yes?"

"Ike, it's Sophie. Captain Hollister called. I told him you were out fishing. He wants to speak with you as soon as possible."

"Did he say why?"

"No, but I sensed he was excited about something. What've you been up to?"

"Quite a lot. Sophie, does the name, Stanley Schaulton, mean anything to you?"

"It *does* sound familiar," she responded slowly. "Schaulton. Stanley Schaulton. Yes! Of course! David used to talk about him—he's the top man at EconoMed."

"Top man?"

"Yes, Ike; he runs the corporation and owns most of the stock. Why?"

Ike decided he'd tell her. "Sophie, for reasons that aren't clear to me, I suspect this Schaulton was probably involved in Natalie's death. Don't ask any questions right now. I've got to get back to Hollister without letting on I'm out of state. I'll call you later." He hung up.

While splashing cold water onto his bruised

face, he thought, *I'd better see if I can identify Dahlia Lennox in that pile first, then call Hollister.*

At mid-pile he found her: *Susan Hayley, 100 E. 68th Street, New York, New York.*

Getting Alonzo Peets on the phone, Ike said, "Lonnie, what can you tell me about Susan Hayley on the upper East Side in the Big Apple?"

"Lemme jes check, ma man." Ike heard his rifling through papers over the phone. "OK, got her. She's a real high-priced ho."

"Ho?" asked Ike.

"Yeh, ho. You know, prositute—she sucks and fucks for bucks. You dig? You want me ta pick her up for you?"

Ike ruminated on this, *It would be smart for me to find out what Hollister's got first.* "No, Lonnie, not right now. Can I get back to you?"

"You da boss, Ikey. Ole Lonnie ain't goan nowhere."

Ike got coffee and Danishes from room service. Swilling the hot liquid in his mouth he contemplated all that was happening, especially curious about what had not happened. *Why hasn't Judy called me?* He had no answer. He showered, dressed and walked across the street to the pay phone on the corner, concerned that somehow Hollister might be able to trace a motel switchboard more easily.

Finally put through to the captain's extension, Ike said, "Hi, this is Ike Darnell."

"Hey, Ike! Got some good fucking news for you. We got some latents off those keys of coke."

"So?" asked Ike, not seeing at all why Hollister sounded so galvanized.

"So we swept that townhouse in Baldwinsville pretty damn good. Somebody tried to wipe it clean, but we found one set of prints—a woman's—on the cold water knob in the shower. They matched."

"Then you believe me?"

"I believed you all along. Right now we're running the prints through the computer. At least we can tie the cocaine in with the townhouse. What we need, though, to get your ass out of a sling is an ID on the prints. If we can locate this foxy lady and get her to sing, we're in business. You catching anything?"

"What?"

"Fishing. You putting many into the fucking boat?"

Ike recovered quickly. "A few. You know how it is."

"Yeh, well you stay put and don't jump bail and we'll get this mess cleaned up. I'll be in touch, Ike."

"No problem," he said to the dead telephone.

Ike cabbed downtown, rang Judy's bell, got no answer, hopped in his Suburban and returned to his room. He called Lonnie Peets and suggested they meet at six o'clock sharp at the corner of Fifth Avenue and Sixty-eighth Street in New York City.

Stanley Schaulton learned by telephone that the New Haven Police had identified the body by virtue of the contents of the Pontiac's trunk. In it they had found Luigi Lente's wallet, forty thousand dollars in cash, a suitcase full of clothes and a hundred .44 Magnum rounds, but no pistol. The police had contacted Schaulton's holding corporation in San Francisco which had, in turn, called him. Schaulton retained a Hartford attorney who faxed a photo of Luigi Lente's mutilated body to him in Dallas.

Stanley Schaulton pondered the photograph.

As though he were ordering a pizza, Schaulton placed a call to an unlisted number in Miami and secured the services of two men.

Their mission: to exterminate Dr. Isaac Darnell.

Ike parked the Suburban in an underground garage on Lexington Avenue, then moseyed over to the corner he had specified. He glanced at his watch: it was 5:45. Ike watched working men and women scurry on this weekday evening back to their posh apartment buildings and condominiums, nod to the liveried doormen and disappear behind walls of glass. Aching and weary, Ike wondered why he had chosen to disengage himself from being a Philadelphia neurosurgeon to do what he was doing, why he was here in New York hunting for a hooker.

He remembered the overwhelming urge he had had in the cemetery. Ike had watched the three coffins lowered into the earth and had, at that moment, felt compelled to leave, to run, to flee all that had been a part of his life. None of it existed any more for him. He had been more surprised than shocked that one man—a nut by the name of Vinny Parisi—could so profoundly change him. Ike saw again the man who was pretending to be a waiter approach the head table, withdraw the gun from his tray, raise it, aim it at him, but this time, Ike was too fast for him. He grabbed the pistol's barrel and pointed it upwards. The first shot struck the track lighting above Ike's head. Harmlessly. Ike swung at the man, connected, beat his awful face, listened to his wife and daughters cheer him on, then—

"Hey, ma man," said Lonnie Peets. "You look lost. Where you been? Neptune?"

"Wha?" Then: "Lonnie!" He shook his old friend's hand, then led him down Sixty-eighth Street, stopping across the road from number one hundred.

"What do you know about this lady, Lonnie?"

"She big time. You gotta call her, tell her who

gave you her number, then ast her for a 'date.'"
Lonnie chuckled. "Ike, I know you got it for free,
but she cost five hundred a night. Anyhow, I called
a few friends in her line a work. I gotta reference.
You gimme the word and I'll use it."

A plan crystallized in Ike's mind. "OK, Lonnie,
you offer her twenty-five hundred—I'm paying—to
go with you to a swanky party tonight in
Greenwich. Tell her anything you want, but just
get her in your car." Ike imaged in his mind the
road he had just traveled. "Pull off at the service
station just past Exit 3 of the Connecticut Turnpike. Tell her you have to go to the john. I'll take it
from there. Got it?"

"Suppose she says she can't make it tonight?"

"Double the money. Tell her you'll pay in
advance. Whatever it takes, you get her there."

Ike accompanied Lonnie into a drug store and
stood by the phone booth. He listened to low volume conversation, then saw Lonnie's thumb pop
up.

Two and a half hours later Ike sat patiently
behind the wheel of the darkened Suburban fifty
yards from the men's room of the Mobil station. He
watched the Rolls Royce Silver Cloud come to a
stop at the curb and smiled as the dapper, well-
dressed, sixtyish black man headed for the
bathroom.

Ike waited until Lonnie exited the men's room, then hopped to the ground and walked slowly towards the passenger side of the Rolls. At the same instant that Lonnie opened the driver's door, Ike entered the back seat. Placing the cold tip of the Magnum pistol to the back of the woman's head, Ike said, "You tell the police the truth, Dahlia honey, and you're going to be just fine."

CHAPTER 9

5 May

Dr. Judy Frymoyer studied the identification shield, then looked at the man's face. She saw a red, booze-ruined complexion, bright hazel eyes, opalescent, even teeth—*no*, she thought, *they're dentures*—a long, hooked nose and a scar on the left cheek. The face matched the picture. The man's body was splendorously covered with a gray, pin-striped suit, white shirt with french cuffs, pearl links and a blue regiment tie, carefully snugged at the collar in a Windsor knot. There was a bulge under his left breast pocket, clearly a weapon. She looked from the gun to the man's scrupulously combed black hair. *He's wearing a toupee*, she thought. "Just why," she asked, finally acknowledging in her mind that the man was who he said he was, "are you interested in Dr. Darnell? Has he committed some federal crime?"

"Yes," said the man purporting himself to be FBI Agent Daniel Stull, "he has fled the jurisdiction of New York State. He was free on bail there until, if our information is correct, two days ago when he came to New Haven. The New York authorities called us in yesterday."

Judy leaned back in the chair behind her designer desk and peered at the man who sat precisely where Ike had yesterday. "How did you get my name?"

"We spoke with Dr. Emelius at the State Medical Society. He informed us that he directed Darnell to you yesterday. Did you meet with him, Dr. Frymoyer?" he asked, suddenly reeling forward and blowing his hot, Binaca-smelling breath across the desk.

My God! thought Judy. *I shouldn't have come right back to the lab yesterday to look for Peter's PG specimens. I lost track of the hours. By the time I called Ike, he'd gone. Where is he? What should I tell this man? The truth? No — then they'd want him for murder. And me as an accessory!* "I met with him," she said.

Stull removed a notebook from his pocket. "When?"

"About two o'clock."

"What did you discuss?"

"A patient," said Judy Frymoyer.

"Name?"

"I'm sorry, Mr. Stull, but that's confidential."

"Surely, Doctor, you don't wish to become involved in this mess yourself?"

"No, I don't," she said, now sweating, "but I must place a patient's rights above all else. As I am sure you know, I took an oath to that effect."

"Of course," said the toupeed man with a cold smile. "I'll be in touch with you." He snatched his black leather shield and left her office.

Outside, he climbed into a rented red Subaru and advised his companion, "She's lying to protect him—probably her too. Let's wait in her apartment. With a bit of persuasion she'll sing."

Detective Captain Bertram Hollister slid Susan Hayley's sworn statement across the glossy conference table. It came to a stop in front of Attorney Arnie Weinstein who read it slowly. "Ike," Weinstein said finally, "with this document, Mrs. Rostikalski's affidavit stating that a pretty black woman directed her to the X-ray Department at Econo-Med and the finding of the corduroy fibers from your trousers on the rug in the townhouse, I believe that our motion for dismissal will be successful."

Relieved, Ike nodded.

"OK, Ike," prodded Hollister, "how did you find her?"

"Is that really important, Captain?"

"No, I'm just fucking curious."

Not responding, Ike arose, shook both men's hands and left.

He obeyed the speed limit meticulously during his drive north to Ogdensburg.

Judy Frymoyer punched the five digit security code into her digital lock and entered her apartment. She set the bag of groceries on the island counter in her kitchen and proceeded into the bathroom for a long, hot soak. While sitting on the toilet lazily emptying her bladder, Judy noted with alarm that the power went off.

In the pitch blackness she heard footsteps, felt strong arms grab her own. Terrified, Judy winced at the prick of a needle, realized she was becoming woozy, was drifting, mumbling, recalling, speaking.

Revealing.

Ike had sat in Dr. Harvey Martin's waiting room for more than an hour. Now, the last patient seen, a nurse beckoned him into the doctor's consultation room, a small dimly lit chamber, floor-to-ceiling book cases flanking an antique cherry rolltop desk. Ike was examining some of the standard medical texts when Dr. Martin came in.

After a brief introduction Ike got right to the point. "Dr. Martin, I come here today with the full permission of Sophie Lepert," he said, proffering a signed authorization to Martin, "to find out details of your treatment of David Lepert."

Harvey Martin, a slightly built, stoop-shouldered man in his mid-forties with a severely receding salt and pepper hairline and a nearly white widow's peak, pushed his reading glasses up to the bridge of his thin nose and examined the document. He flipped it onto his desk, then pressed the intercom button and requested that David Lepert's medical record be brought to him. "What do you want to know?"

"I understand that you were administering allergy immunotherapy injections to Mr. Lepert."

"Correct," said Martin. "He was severely allergic to house dust and mold spores—had debilitating symptoms of rhinitis and asthma. He was responding nicely to treatment right up until he developed his other problems, first the leukemia, then the Alzheimer's. David Lepert was a most unfortunate man," he said, a sad, compassionate look on his face. "I continued his shots nonetheless, but by then, his respiratory disorders were insignificant."

"I take it," said Ike, "that you referred him to an allergist for work-up."

"Yes. John Felske in Watertown. He's Econo-Med's man in this area. Frankly, he's damned good, a shrewd clinician with superb acumen. Felske doesn't miss much. He skin and blood tested David and created an allergenic extract which he sent to me with a schedule for administration of the shots. I followed his instructions to the letter."

"What was the composition of that extract?" asked Ike.

Martin fished a sheet from the chart in his hands and scanned it. "Fifty per cent house dust, fifty percent mold mix."

"What company provided the raw materials for those solutions?"

Martin's eyes drifted downward to the paper. "Stiles Laboratories. It's a nationwide outfit with headquarters in Dallas. They have an exclusive contract with EconoMed to supply allergenic extracts for all participants who require them." Martin massaged his temples thoughtfully with a slim index finger and thumb. "Now that you mention it, Dr. Darnell, I seem to recall that David's daughter asked me these very same questions six, maybe eight, months before she died. She asked for samples of Mr. Lepert's serum. I gave them to her. To this day I still don't know why she wanted or what she did with them."

Excited, Ike asked, "Do you still have those vials?"

"Yep—all five of them. In my refrigerator so the proteins don't denature."

"Five?"

"Yes, the standard treatment set consists of vials 'A' through 'E,' each successive one ten times more concentrated than the one before. We usually give five shots from each vial at weekly intervals. By the time we get up to vial 'E,' we begin to increase to every two weeks, then every three, then once a month."

Ike found himself considering this information with the cold aloofness of a clinician, judging its merit, its scientific accuracy. Then, realizing that Natalie Lepert's suspicions regarding this very treatment had probably resulted in her murder, Ike asked, "Tell me, Dr. Martin, have you noticed any unusual problems with this type of therapy in any of your other patients?"

Martin rubbed his knuckles studiously on the stubble on his chin. "Like what?"

"Like adverse reactions. Anything unexplainable which might have happened to these patients—that sort of thing."

"No," Martin said finally. "I've had what I believe are the expected number of local reactions, usually large red swellings, not unlike huge hives. And, maybe once or twice a year a patient of mine will have a systemic anaphylactic reaction—diffuse hives, wheezing, shock, the whole bit. That's why we keep them in the office for a half hour or so. Remember, we're giving them injections of proteins which they're allergic to. Over the course of several months of treatment the patient develops immunological tolerance to these proteins. That's why they get better." Martin paused. "But, no, Dr. Darnell, I am not aware of any other sequelae to these allergy shots."

"Would you mind," asked Ike, "if I took Mr. Lepert's serum for analysis?"

"Certainly not. I've been meaning to clean out all of the inactive patients' vials for some time now. You can have the lot if you like."

Ike Darnell smiled. "Yes, I'd like that. And if you think of anything, please contact me."

Ike left the family doctor's office carrying a large cardboard box.

The man who had identified himself as FBI Agent Daniel Stull placed the barrel of his .38 snub-nose against the black man's temple and pulled the trigger. He allowed the body to fall across the front seat of the silver Rolls Royce, then walked across the Wildwood sand dune and got into the red Subaru.

"Where to?" asked the plump neckless man behind the wheel.

"Syracuse," said Dante Callanti.

Judy Frymoyer awakened fully clothed on her bed. She tried desperately to remember what had happened to her. Her mind still fuzzy, as though, she thought, from drink, Judy could recall only brief moments from earlier this evening.

She rolled off the bed and attempted to stand, but her legs did not hold her and she fell. Reaching up in the blackness, she remembered the power outage which had occurred before whatever happened to her. Finding her bedside lamp she twisted the switch, not really expecting it to work.

The room exploded with light.

She felt between her legs and realized that she had not been raped. Glancing about her, Judy saw her jewelry on the dresser and knew that she had not been robbed.

What happened? she asked herself.

The single syllable, *Ike,* flashed into the forefront of her brain. Then the smell of Binaca. She remembered the FBI Agent and realized that, in the heart of her darkness, she had smelled his breath once again. That was in her memory; what he had said was not—only that it had something to do, as the first time, with Ike Darnell.

Judy Frymoyer picked up her telephone and dialed the Directory Assistance Operator for Ogdensburg, New York.

Dr. Harvey Martin, wearing his pajamas and bathrobe, sat at the computer terminal in his study. He switched on his modem and made the connection with his office computer. A nagging suspicion had prevented his sleeping and had compelled him to do what he was doing.

Twenty minutes later, his search of memory completed, Martin tiptoed into his bedroom so as not to disturb his snoring wife and extracted from his suit jacket the paper Ike had given him.

Returning to his study he sat in a light blue Lazy-Boy and lifted the receiver of his telephone.

At eleven PM New York State Trooper Randy Truman interrupted his fantasy of a salacious blow job by the night waitress at the Tinker Tavern off Exit 35 to train his radar gun on a speeding red Subaru. He squeezed the trigger.

79 flashed on his screen.

His emergency lights flickering, Truman roared off the grassy divider and gave chase. The Subaru's speed increased. He activated his siren and floored the accelerator.

Four miles south of Syracuse on I-81 the Subaru rolled to a stop on the shoulder. Trooper Truman sauntered to the car's driver's window and leaned on the roof.

The single .38 round killed him instantly.

Ike Darnell didn't realize that he'd accidentally kicked his phone off the hook until he'd stepped out of the shower in his motel room and was toweling off. He stood there blotting the moisture from his body when a warm breeze assailed him through the open window. *My God!* he thought, *it's a lot warmer out than I'd estimated earlier. I can't leave those vials in the car until morning. I've got to get dressed, run down to Sophie's and put them into her refrigerator. Tomorrow I'll get in touch with Judy and make arrangements for her to analyze them.*

Ike knew that, for reasons not clear to him yet, Natalie Lepert had met her demise because of her concerns about the contents of these bottles. Every clue he'd uncovered pointed in that direction. *But what was so goddamned important about them?* he wondered. *What is the meaning of Peter Tillers' abbreviation "PG"? What has it to do with David Lepert's allergy serum? With EconoMed? With Dahlia Lennox? With Harold Hutchins? With Stanley Schaulton?*

Ike dressed pensively. He replaced the telephone receiver, left his motel room and hopped into the blue Suburban.

Detective Captain Bertram Hollister brought his unmarked Dodge to a screeching halt fifty yards from the crime scene. He walked over to the prostrate body and stared into the glazed open eyes of the boyish face. The police photographer's flash indelibly engraved that vacant horror into his memory. A brief interview with the investigator already on the scene revealed that a passing trucker had seen a red Subaru pull away from that spot, even as the Trooper was falling. Hollister learned that the murderer had proceeded directly into

Syracuse — where the trucker had lost it — and that was why he'd been called.

The captain returned to his vehicle and radioed this information into headquarters, requesting that any vehicle even remotely fitting that description should be stopped and approached with extreme caution.

Hollister seethed as he drove slowly through the dimly lit city streets. Murder always angered him; cop-killing made him furious. He parked and entered the station.

The desk sergeant looked up from his crossword puzzle as Hollister approached. "Captain," he said, "a guy was just here looking for you — said he wanted to talk with that black doctor, Darnell. You just missed him."

Hollister paused and pursed his lips. "He identify himself?"

"Yep. He said he was one of Darnell's colleagues and heard he'd been in some trouble and wanted to help. He left his card. Here," the sergeant said, extending the white rectangle to Hollister, who read: *Daniel Callison, M.D.* with a New York City address.

"What'd he look like?" asked Hollister.

"Tall, black toupee, duded up in a three piece suit, scar on his left cheek."

Hollister considered these words. "Did you make him for a doctor?"

"Now that you mention it, Captain, no. He looked like a real slick hood."

"What'd you fucking tell him?"

"The name of Darnell's motel up in Ogdensburg."

Though it was late, Harvey Martin called John Felske's home number in Watertown. He had tried Ike Darnell's motel room for more than an hour, first getting a busy signal, then no answer. Astonished at his discovery and anxious to share it, Martin felt that the allergist who had prescribed the treatment should be one of the first to know.

"Hello?"

"John, it's Harvey Martin in Ogdensburg. There's something you should be aware of." He explained the results of his computer inquiries.

Felske ended the conversation with: "OK, Harvey. Let me sleep on it. First thing in the morning I'll call the EconoMed Allergy Chief in Dallas and discuss it with him. I'll get back to you."

Sophie Lepert answered the door in her red velvet bathrobe. "Ike! Come on in. I've been trying to reach you for the past hour." Ike entered carrying a cardboard box. "What's that?" asked Sophie.

"Allergy serum. Some of it David's. Do you mind if I put them in your refrigerator?"

"Certainly not. Ike, a woman by the name of

Judy Frymoyer has been calling here every ten minutes since ten-thirty. She wants you to call her. Says it's an emergency. Here's the num—"

Ike picked up the ringing telephone and spoke fervently with Judy Frymoyer for four minutes. He snatched up the box he'd set on the hall table and said, "Sophie, do you have a cooler? One of those things you'd take on a picnic?"

"Sure do. Why?"

"I'm not going to leave this stuff here. I'm taking it with me and it must be kept cool."

"Where are you going at this hour?"

"New Haven." Ike paused. "Sophie, I believe that the key to why Natalie was murdered—and possibly by whom—may lie in this box."

"Explain," she implored.

He did so while dumping ice cubes into the red, white and blue cooler.

Stanley Schaulton was wide awake sipping scotch when his private line rang. "Yes?"

"It's me," said Dante Callanti, the high-priced Miami hit-man who had murdered more than two hundred human beings in cold blood during the past thirty years and had never been caught. He stood in a phone booth on a deserted street in Alexandria Bay, thirty miles from Ogdensburg. "I should make contact with our client within the hour."

"Superb," cooed Schaulton.

"Do you want his body found or should I pull a Hoffa?"

Without hesitating, the CEO of EconoMed International said, "The latter—and make it clean."

CHAPTER 10

6 May

Captain Bertram Hollister roared down South Salina Street, turned into the McDonald's parking lot and stopped his vehicle next to the abandoned red Subaru. He walked slowly around the car, notebook in hand, recording the vehicle ID number, plate number and every other relevant detail. Seven minutes later, with the assistance of the computer man at the station, Hollister had determined that the Subaru had been rented the previous day in New Haven, Connecticut by a man who had paid cash in advance for one week and who had presented a Georgia driver's license in the name of Dieter Callender, age fifty-one, 1010 Peachtree Place, Atlanta.

Hollister assisted his forensic man, Eddie Modeck, in working up the vehicle. To his naked eye it was clean except for fourteen Marlboro cigarette butts in the back seat ashtray. After dusting the entire interior and exterior for prints, Hollister and Modeck vacuumed the upholstery and carpets, sealing the detritus from each sector in a separate bag.

By nine-twenty AM, eighty minutes after he had found the Subaru, Hollister was back at his office and knew that Trooper Truman's prints were on the roof above the driver's door, that 1010 Peachtree Place was a public park and that Dieter Callender had been reported missing to the Atlanta police by his family four months ago.

At nine-fifty-three Hollister received a fax of the New Haven car rental agent's statement. Mr. Callender, according to the agent, had been a well-dressed man with a black wig and a scar on his left cheek.

The Captain telephoned Ike Darnell's motel in Ogdensburg, learning that Darnell was out.

He dialed Sophie Lepert's number. Waiting for her to answer, he thought, *This fucking thing is starting to stink and stink real bad. What the hell has Ike to do with a cop-killer?* Though Hollister had no explanation, he knew somehow that the connection was the same one that had linked Ike with a slick, black, New York hooker and a bogus cocaine rap.

The phone continued to ring in his ear. When it was clear to Hollister that his call would not be answered, he developed a sick feeling in his gut. He knew, via his cop's sixth sense, that something was dreadfully wrong.

Speeding north on I-81 towards Ogdensburg, the Captain glanced at his watch. It was 10:01 AM.

Judy Frymoyer reclined naked under her covers desultorily stroking Ike Darnell's buttocks. She had never thought of herself as an easy lay, but was simply overpowered by the seemingly exhausted man who had arrived at her apartment at six o'clock this morning.

She remembered fixing him coffee, listening to his animated account of his activities since their parting yesterday, making up the couch for him to sleep, then wilting in his strong arms at his first touch. After their first coupling, while Ike slept, Judy called in to her office, indicating that she would be delayed and to cancel her morning's schedule. Ike had awakened clearly aroused and they had done it again. Now, wide-eyed and alert, Judy listened to his rhythmic breathing and, dancing her fingertips over his sexy behind, wondered how her peaceful existence as a Yale allergist had been sucked into this maelstrom of murder and urgent, frenetic copulation.

Judy's entire body tingled, especially her nipples and her clitoris, and she realized that the whys and wherefores were of no import. She knew that she was living, *really living*, for the first time in years and that's all that mattered at the moment.

She slipped out of bed and into a robe. Smiling, she looked forward to surprising her lover with a first-rate breakfast.

Judy switched on the Coffee-Mate and opened the refrigerator. She eyed the eggs, bacon, milk, butter, orange juice and the small, clear vials of amber liquids.

Dante Callanti descended the five steps from the front door of the Lepert residence in Ogdensburg and trotted up the block, getting in to the white Cadillac Fleetwood Brougham he had stolen from a Syracuse dealership's lot last night.

"Did she talk?" asked his driver.

"Yes," said Callanti, lighting a Marlboro. "Darnell went back to New Haven to meet with that lady doctor."

The driver started the car. "Ja kill her?"

"Not exactly," said Callanti. "Let's make some tracks to Utica. I know a man there who can give us a clean car. We should be in New Haven by tonight."

"You gonna just waltz in that apartment and pop em?" asked the driver.

"That's my job, Pizzi. Let's go. It's almost noon."

Hollister stopped at Ike's motel first and verified that he was gone, then sped into town, stopping in front of Sophie Lepert's home. He stood there for several minutes under the early afternoon sun, pounding on the front door before he realized it was unlocked.

A chill bristled down his spine. Hollister withdrew his pistol, crouched and gently pushed open the tall oak portal. Inside the vestibule he listened carefully, not breathing, but heard no sound.

Small steps took him into the library. It was empty. Quickly he walked into each ground floor room with the same result.

Bertram Hollister found Sophie Lepert's viciously beaten body upstairs in her laundry room, stuffed into the dryer. He felt her carotid pulse. She was alive. He touched the inside of the dryer. It was hot.

As Hollister waited for the ambulance to come, he realized that he wasn't dealing just with a pro. Any man who would beat up an old lady, then cram her into a dryer and turn it on was sick. Hollister knew they didn't come any worse than a sick pro.

He suddenly realized that Natalie Lepert—the girl he had found dead in bed almost three years ago—had grown up in this house. Hollister stared at the dryer, saw it spin around in his mind, saw the mother's face, the daughter's, Ike's, the hooker's, the glassy eyes of the young, dead Trooper.

The police detective was snapped from his confused, tragic thoughts by a voice.

He heard the beaten old woman articulate softly, through her swollen mouth and broken teeth, "Dr. Frymoyer . . . Yale . . . message pad," then saw her slump back into unconsciousness.

After Sophie Lepert had been taken to the local hospital, but before the local police had arrived, Hollister found the name and phone number scrawled on the yellow pad next to the hall phone.

He ripped off the top sheet and exited into the sunshine.

Hollister used the pay phone in the emergency room at the EconoMed Clinic. On the second ring a machine answered. He left a brief message, then sought out the doctor on duty, hoping that Mrs. Lepert was not as seriously injured as she'd appeared.

Dr. Judy Frymoyer's laboratory would have been the envy of any immunologist. She had, courtesy of Yale University and numerous grants from the National Institutes of Health and the National Science Foundation, every device necessary to fractionate and purify complex protein molecules.

Ike Darnell peered over Judy's shoulder at the vacillating stylus which traced a spike on a graph each time a different chemical species passed through the sensor of her electrophoretic chromatography apparatus. Ike had been amazed at Judy's perspicacity in evaluating the problem of how properly to analyze David Lepert's allergy serum and that of Dr. Martin's other patients so as to generate results of a similar nature to Peter Tillers'. She had explained to him that Tillers had done this same protein separation and, extrapolating from Tillers' data, she could pinpoint the one he had designated "PG." Judy's review of Tillers' meticulous notes had revealed to her that "PG" was not a prostaglandin, but a protein of very high molecular weight—probably an antigen or an antibody.

Ike was silent as Judy collected in a test tube two cc's of a clear solution from the tip of the chromatographic column and labeled it "House Dust Mite Protein, *Dermatophagoides farinae.*" Ten minutes later she bottled a similar sample.

"Is that it?" asked Ike.

"Yes." She wrote "PG" on the red and white sticker.

"Now what?" Ike had excised many tumors and many bullets from many brains, but he knew little about the nuts and bolts of immunochemistry.

"We must determine PG's biological activity. My plan is to inject a dozen Rhesus monkeys on a regular basis—much as we give allergy patients shots—with this material, then monitor the animals clinically. If PG is an antigen, then we should see a corresponding rise in antibody titers. If it's an antibody, then we should be able to detect some target organ effect."

All of Ike's experiences since the day he'd answered the ad in *The New England Journal of Medicine* flashed into his mind. He shook his head, hoping his ignorance didn't show. "Is it possible, Judy, that this PG caused David Lepert's leukemia? Or his Alzheimer's?"

Judy placed her hand on his shoulder. "Anything is possible, Ike, when you're dealing with the immune system."

"But why? Why would any physician purposefully make his patient worse?"

"That, my dear, I cannot even guess at."

Judy repeated the process on the serum of another of Harvey Martin's patients, then led Ike into her animal room where they systematically injected twenty-four squealing Rhesus monkeys.

They dined at an Italian restaurant two blocks from Judy's apartment, then returned there, smiles on their faces.

Out of habit, after double-locking her door, Judy rewound her answering machine tape. She pressed the play button.

The words of Bertram Hollister were even and measured, revealing alarm only in their undertones: "Ike, it's Bert Hollister. You must—I repeat, you must—leave there immediately. I have reason to believe that a man is following you, a man who murdered a cop, then beat Sophie Lepert near death to learn your whereabouts. Get to a safe place with Dr. Frymoyer, then call me at my office. I'm not there, but they'll know where to reach me. Good-bye, my friend."

Dante Callanti screwed the silencer onto his nine millimeter Mauser. He stepped out of his green Buick onto the black tar of the parking lot of Judy Frymoyer's apartment building, keeping his eyes peeled on the bright lights visible through the sixteenth floor windows. Callanti walked deliberately towards the fire door in the rear of the building, then stopped suddenly when the lights went out all at once.

He eyed the black windows and smiled, thinking, *They're either going to sleep or screwing. This'll be a piece of cake.* Picking the lock with ease, Callanti entered the staircase at basement level and ascended the steps slowly to the penthouse.

Seconds later, gun poised at the ready, he entered Judy Frymoyer's apartment. Hearing a television blasting from the bedroom, Callanti inched his way towards the noise. The door was open. He felt for the wall switch and flicked it on.

The room was empty.

A rapid search revealed that his marks were gone.

Ike drove Judy's Porche out of the underground garage into the sparse traffic of the Oak Street Connector, then pulled onto the entrance ramp to the Connecticut Turnpike. He sped north towards Hartford.

"Where are we going?" asked Judy.

"I know a place," said Ike Darnell.

Though Sophie Lepert's injuries were severe, Bertram Hollister was relieved that her doctors felt she would survive.

He left the EconoMed Clinic in Ogdensburg and proceeded directly to the local police station to give his statement. Entering the municipal building, Hollister became aware immediately that the local blues were in a state of chaos.

"What's up?" he asked a mustaschioed cop who was writing a report at the front counter.

The cop looked up at him absently. "Coupla guys were out fishin this afternoon on the St. Lawrence. Their boat went down and they drowned. We just pulled the bodies out of the drink."

"Oh," said Hollister reticently. "Who were they?"

"Two doctors—one local, the other from Watertown. Martin and Felske. The chief's notifying their families right now.

The names didn't register. "That's too bad," said Bertram Hollister.

CHAPTER 11

7 May

Judy Frymoyer lowered her exhausted body onto the broad, flat rock at the edge of the Dennys River. She thrust her head back and, peering through closed eyes into the brilliant morning sun, wondered how she'd managed to come so far from where she'd been.

Judy had grown up in a fashionable suburb of Boston, one where her father, a black attorney — and later a judge — and his attractive family had had no difficulty assimilating. After Radcliffe College and Harvard Medical School she'd gone on to an allergy fellowship at the University of Chicago, then had been picked up by Yale as a junior faculty member. After eight years, retirements of several senior men, then the unexpected death of the Chief, she'd been promoted to Acting Chief, later full Chief, of the Allergy and Immunology service at Yale School of Medicine.

Judy flicked a dragon fly from her forearm and mused that her life had been so placid, so even — until the day a man named Ike Darnell had entered it. Now she had practically been the accomplice to a murder and was being pursued by some unknown individual whose mission it was to kill the man she thought she couldn't live without.

She remembered their long drive from Connecticut to rural Maine. Ike had stopped in Bangor to telephone the Syracuse Police Detective, then had driven into the wilderness, certain, he had said, that he could find the little cabin on the little river which he had visited with his wife fifteen years ago.

Judy watched an Atlantic salmon (Salmo salar, she thought) fly into the air on its way upstream. She smiled. Ike had found the place he was looking for, even the hidden key under the third brick from the left rear of the chimney, precisely where his old friend, Jeremy Chess, a Philadelphia pathologist, had told him it would be, should he ever wish to visit.

Feeling somehow more awake, though she had not slept much in the car, Judy got up and walked up the gentle slope to the quaint cabin. She ducked her head in the door and heard Ike snoring, then hopped into the Porche. She had seen a pay phone several miles back on the main road.

Judy looked at her watch, pulling to a stop at the telephone. 9:45 AM. She wondered if Dennysville, Maine was in the same time zone as New Haven, Connecticut. She placed her quarters in the slot and dialed her office number.

After two rings: "Dr. Frymoyer's office. May I help you?"

"Alice, it's me," she said to her laboratory technician-*cum*-receptionist.

"DR. FRYMOYER! Where have you been? I've been calling your apartment for the past hour. You've got six patients in rooms ready to be seen and they're not pleased. Also, Mrs. Schottenberg called about ten minutes ago. Lisa's having another bad asthma attack and she's bringing her in to the ER right now."

"Alice, I've had a family emergency and am not in New Haven. Please get Dr. Burke to see Lisa and any other emergencies and please cancel all of my office appointments for the rest of the week."

"What happened?" asked Alice Hyde, *sotte voce*.

"I really can't elaborate. I'm sorry; I'll explain when I get back. I want you to call Dean Palmer and apprise him of my sudden leave. Further, Alice—and this is critical—there are two vials in the green refrigerator, second shelf. They're labeled

'PG-1' and 'PG-2.' They're to be administered to the Rhesus monkeys specified in the protocol sheet in my laboratory ledger from yesterday. Only there's one difference: instead of one day intervals between successively higher dosages, give them six hours apart. Do you understand?"

"Yes."

"Good. I'll call you back tomorrow." Judy hung up, then, at the operator's request, deposited more coins into the slots.

On her way back to the Dennys River, Judy Frymoyer thought, *I've never done anything like this in my whole life — but this guy's worth it.*

Bertram Hollister set down his telephone. Astonished at what he had learned from his stockbroker, he picked up the phone and called information for Dallas, Texas. A mechanical voice spat the number at him in strange monosyllables; he jotted it down, then dialed.

"Good morning. EconoMed International. May I help you?" a cheery female voice said.

"I'd like to know how to reach one of your subsidiaries," said Hollister.

"Which one?"

"Stiles Laboratories."

"No problem, sir. It's this same number, extension four-seven-oh-three. I'll be happy to connect you."

"Thank you," said Hollister before hanging up.

Oh, my God! he thought. *Ike was absolutely right! He told me he suspected that the connection between Natalie Lepert and her murderer was her father's allergy shots—made from extracts produced by Stiles Labs. But Ike didn't have any idea how or why they were related. I know how, but not why.* The detective congratulated himself for thinking to call Merrill Lynch and ask his old buddy, Jimmy Olasker, to get him the lowdown on both corporations, learning that they were one and the same.

But why? What the fuck is this 'PG' bullshit Ike's talking about? And how precisely is this mealymouthed asshole, Harold Hutchins, involved in all this crap? Hollister knew that he had to talk at length with Ike Darnell and Judy Frymoyer, but that he would simply have to wait. Ike had said he'd call sometime this evening. Hollister would bounce this little tidbit off of him and see what he had to say.

What did Natalie Lepert know, wondered Hollister, *that forced somebody to kill her?*

He was roused from his thoughts by a knock on his door. The messenger handed him a large envelope from the FBI lab in D.C. Hollister opened it.

The fingerprints on the Marlboro butts had matched the ones on the phony doctor's business card. Hollister knew this.

His jaw dropped when he looked at the second page.

135

Twenty-one years ago, the FBI had recovered a single thumbprint from a weapon used in a gangland-style murder in Louisiana. Eye-witness accounts and some physical evidence had suggested that the perpetrator was the infamous assassin, known to the agency only as "The Cue Ball," a reference to the man's alleged baldness.

No match had ever been found. No clue existed as to the man's identity.

Until today.

The Cue Ball had touched the Marlboros, the business card and the pistol found in the New Orleans union hall.

And now, realized Hollister, that person was hunting Dr. Isaac Darnell.

Stanley Schaulton made no effort to hide his fury. He spat into the receiver, "You're gonna find those two doctors, Danny boy, and you're going to find them fast." He paused. Dante Callanti, hundreds of miles away, sitting in a New Haven hotel room, said nothing into his telephone.

"I have taken the liberty," continued Schaulton, "of learning the credit card numbers of all accounts held by both of them, then reporting them to a reliable man of mine who is appropriately placed. Within twenty-four hours of the use of one of those cards—even for a tank of gas—I'll know it. You stay right where you are. I'll be in touch, my friend."

Unable to find a pair of bathing trunks that fit, Ike jumped naked into the cold swirling river. He submerged, swam to the other bank underwater, then was pleasantly surprised to bump into Judy on his way back. She was similarly attired.

Thirty seconds later Ike scampered out, shivering. Judy followed. Comforted now by his towel and basking in the deliciously warm sunlight, Ike gazed into Judy's liquid brown eyes. A blue heron swooped down behind him and came up with a bass, but Ike didn't see it.

He placed his hand gently upon her thigh. "You sorry you got mixed up in all of this?" he asked.

Judy blushed, her caramel skin becoming chocolate brown. "Forty-eight hours ago I was a respectable allergist at Yale University. Now I'm sunbathing in the raw in the Maine wilderness with a brain surgeon who thinks he's James Bond."

Ike nodded.

"My answer is yes and no. I'm happy to be with you and I'm pleased that we might have a grasp on why your Dr. Lepert and my Dr. Tillers were killed—but I'm disappointed in myself for giving up everything I've spent my life working for on what can only be called a whim, a spur-of-the-moment decision."

Ike tongued her nipple. It rose to meet him. "Any regrets?" he asked.

"No. You?"

He buried his face in her belly and wetted her navel with his burning lips. "None."

After making love with a passion he had thought was the province of teenagers, Ike said, "Let's make ourselves more presentable, drive into one of these towns and get something to eat."

"Great idea! I'm famished. But we haven't got much cash."

"No problem. We'll put it on plastic. Let's get a move on. After dinner I want to call Hollister."

They dined at the Banning House just off Route One.

Before dessert, Ike phoned Hollister. It was eight-fifteen. Stunned by the ten minute conversation, he returned to their table.

Judy handed him his gold American Express card. "Take this back, my friend. I found I had enough cash and paid. The dinner's on me." She smiled broadly and, wetting the tip of her little finger in her mouth, thrust it into the vanilla ice cream, then touched Ike's lips.

Feeling himself grow hard in an instant, Ike lapped up the whiteness with his tongue. "You know, lady, after a gesture like that, it's unlikely you'll get much sleep tonight."

Judy roared with laughter, her ripe, brown bosoms rippling beneath her light cotton blouse, her white teeth flashing. She grasped his thigh under the table and squeezed.

In the midst of telling her Bertram Hollister's revelation, Ike arose and led Judy out to the car. Neither slept much, but both well.

CHAPTER 12

8 May

Alice Hyde entered Dr. Frymoyer's laboratory shortly after six AM. She had established a dosing regimen of six, noon, six and midnight. Her boss had said this experiment was "critical." She would do it right.

Alice opened the refrigerator, withdrew the vials and prepared the injections, then carried the tray of loaded syringes into the animal room. Flipping on the bright, fluorescent overhead lights, she studied carefully the two dozen monkeys. They appeared fidgety as usual and some snorted and hissed at her, but none seemed to have been overtly affected by whatever "PG" was. She gave the shots, wondering all the while, what type of experiment she was conducting.

Sophie Lepert awakened in the midst of a horrid dream. She could see herself, as though an observer, absorb punch after brutal punch from the crazed, bald man with the funny looking wig. She heard the man shriek his questions at the bloodied woman on the laundry room floor, kick her, strangle her, command her to tell him where Ike Darnell was.

Then the pain assaulted her from every corner of her body and she knew it was no dream.

She opened her swollen eyes and stared into the grizzled, red face of Detective Captain Bertram Hollister, recognizing him immediately.

"Where am I, Captain?" she murmured.

"Safe, sound and alive in the hospital in Syracuse. They transferred you here last night for neurological consultation. You were semicomatose and they needed to do a CAT scan."

"I was beaten," she said, making it a question by raising her eyebrows.

"Yes," said Hollister gravely. "You were beaten to within an inch of your life. I just spoke with your doctors. They think you're going to be fine."

Sophie glanced at the casts on her legs and left arm. "Fine?"

"In time, yes. Fine."

"And Ike?" she asked.

"Is safe in hiding. There's a very bad man after him, Mrs. Lepert. A very bad man."

"The guy who did this?" She gestured with her unfettered right arm.

"Yes."

"God help him, Captain."

"God and me, Mrs. Lepert. You get some rest. I'll stop in to see you later."

At dawn Ike drove the Porche onto the ferry boat at Eastport. He and Judy clung to each other at the railing watching silently as the frigid waters of the Cobscook Bay swished by. Ike thought of the plan Hollister had outlined to him on the phone: *We've got to draw him in, Ike. I've called the feds and they believe me—fingerprints don't lie. This guy's a real big boy. Only for some reason he's being fucking sloppy now. You leave the cabin, go fifty, maybe a hundred miles away and stay put. The FBI will surround that place. There'll be a fucking armed agent behind every rock and every tree. Tomorrow we spring the trap. The trigger man shows and we nail his ass.*

The ferry docked at Deer Island. Ike pulled onto the shore and waited for the boat to St. Andrews, New Brunswick. He thought it would be a nice, quiet place to spend a few days.

Ike had told Judy every word Hollister had said. Now she broke the silence: "Ike, honey, I really don't understand Captain Hollister's plan. How is he going to get this goon to come to Dennysville, Maine?"

Ike shook his head. "Beats me. He didn't want us to know anything about that. His orders were simple—get the hell out of there, but leave our clothes and some personal effects in the cabin and be seen at the general store in town. We're following his instructions to the letter."

"Do you comprehend what's happening to us?" asked Judy, a touch of fear in her voice.

Ike watched the St. Andrews ferry dock and started his engine. "Judy, we've both been trained to think logically and consequentially, to reason things through—that's what medicine is all about. So let's examine the facts. Three years after her death, I start prying into why Natalie Lepert was murdered—and there's no question in my mind that somebody killed her. The trail leads to this Hutchins character at EconoMed, to a guy who was helping her analyze house dust extracts, then to Peter Tillers and you. A New York hooker sets me up, then a slug working for the head of Econo-Med tries to kill me. Then somebody—probably Schaulton again—puts a big-league hit man on my trail. The guy beats the snot out of Sophie Lepert, finds out where I am, then loses us in New Haven. You isolate 'PG' and begin experimentation. We don't know what the heck it really is, just that it appears to be the key to the whole shooting match." Ike paused. "No, I don't have a good grasp on the big picture, but my gut instinct tells me that the results of your lab studies will bring everything into focus. Agree?"

Judy was silent as Ike eased his way onto the boat. Then: "It *is* sound thinking. When we get to a phone I'll call my tech. What worries me is that, if, in fact, 'PG' has some significant biological effect, it may take weeks, months or years to see it. Remember, it takes a long time for allergy shots to be effective. It's also possible that this 'PG' thing may be a wild goose chase."

"I doubt it. People don't hire professional hit men for nothing. I think they're afraid of what we might find."

Ike drove into the center of St. Andrews. While Ike was tanking up at a Mobil station, Judy called Alice Hyde in New Haven: "Alice, how's it going? Anything to report?"

"No, Doctor. The animals are tolerating the shots well with no apparent side effects. Just what are you looking for?"

"I'm not really sure," said Frymoyer. "That's why I'm calling. I want you to take blood specimens from each of the monkeys and run immunoglobulin electrophoreses and complete blood profiles on them. If there's an unusual protein being produced, then that may be significant."

"You seem rushed," stated Alice.

"I am."

"Then why don't we accelerate the dosing—say,

give the increasing dosages every one or two hours?"

Judy mulled this over. "Good idea. Make the interval between shots hourly—a dozen dosages a day from six AM to five PM. Might you have some preliminary results by tomorrow?"

"Probably," said Alice Hyde.

"Good. I'll call you then." Judy rang off, used the ladies' room, then returned to the car just as Ike was signing the charge slip for the gasoline.

Dante Callanti, rudely awakened from his sleep, snatched up the ringing telephone. He heard: "Hiya, Danny boy. We've got a fix on him. Earlier today," said Stanley Schaulton, "Isaac Darnell, M.D. filled up a red Porche registered to Judith Frymoyer, M.D. in a little Canadian town called St. Andrews in New Brunswick."

"When?" asked Callanti.

"Ten AM."

"Where's the nearest airport?" said the killer.

"Fredericton, New Brunswick. It's about sixty miles away. Fly there immediately. Go to the Hertz counter and ask for the package for Tom Engels. In it will be all you'll need. *Capishe?*"

"Yes."

"And, Danny boy?"

"Yes?"

"Don't screw this up," said Stanley Schaulton before breaking the connection.

Bertram Hollister left Sophie Lepert's room on 4-B of the EconoMed Clinic in Syracuse and took the elevator down to the main lobby. He looked up at the huge clock on the wall. 4:20. *Good*, thought Hollister, *he'll still be there*. The detective was anxious to set his plan into motion.

He rode up to the eleventh floor of the professional building and entered Harold Hutchins' receptionist's office without knocking. "Excuse me," he said to the gray-haired lady who sat at the desk typing, "is Dr. Hutchins in?"

The woman peered up at him. She hesitated, then smiled. "May I tell him your name?"

"Hollister."

She made a brief call, then led him into the pathologist's office.

Hollister strode over to the desk and extended his hand. "Good afternoon, Doctor. It's been a long time."

"Yes, Captain, it has," said Hutchins, his face marked by confusion and concern. "What brings you here?"

"A fellow by the name of Ike Darnell. Know him?"

"We've met," said Hutchins suspiciously.

"Then you know that Darnell has been investigating the death of Dr. Natalie Lepert."

"Yes."

Hollister paused to light a Camel, then, puffing great clouds of smoke, he asked, "You mind if I smoke?"

Hutchins shook his head and produced an ashtray from a drawer, sliding it across the desk.

"You know, Doctor, Darnell called me yesterday and told me he thinks he's identified Natalie Lepert's killer."

Hollister saw Hutchins' lips tremble and heard him say indignantly, "Damnit! Are we going to get on that merry-go-round again? It was natural causes. There was no evidence of murder. Certainly both you and Darnell have read the necropsy report I submitted."

Hollister puffed the ash red hot, allowing its tip to fall on Hutchins' blotter. "That's the problem, Doctor. Darnell thinks the killer's name is Harold Hutchins."

The pathologist blanched. Beads of perspiration dotted his upper lip. "You're joking, of course."

"He says he's got evidence," said Hollister equably. "He wanted me to meet him to review it."

"Are you here to arrest me, Captain?"

"No. To warn you. I believe Darnell's a fucking whacko. I don't think he's got jackshit." Hollister extracted several small sheets of note paper from his shirt pocket and set them on the desk before him. Glancing at the top one, he said, "He called me this morning from some tiny fucking town in Maine where he's banging some lady doctor friend of his. Says he's sorted through his notes and has it all figured—that you were balling Natalie, she threatened to sing to your wife, you offed her and covered with a phony autopsy. Any truth to it?" Hollister raised his eyes from the paper.

After a silence, Hutchins said, "No. None."

"That's what I thought. A man of your stature should be aware of crap like this," said the police detective, as he snatched his papers from the desk and stood up.

It was as he was extending his right hand to shake Hutchins' that Hollister allowed one paper to slip from his left and fall onto the carpet.

Immediately after Hollister had left, Harold Hutchins' mind raced, mulling over this astounding information. He walked out to his waiting room and dismissed his secretary. En route to the private telephone in his desk drawer, he saw and picked up the paper Hollister had dropped.

Stanley Schaulton picked up on the second ring. "Yes?"

"It's Hutchins. I know where Darnell is."

Schaulton smiled. "Where?"

"A fishing camp in a place called Dennysville, Maine."

Schaulton pictured the map in his mind and suddenly realized that St. Andrews, New Brunswick was right on the Maine border. But he had no idea where Dennysville was. "How did you come by this information, Hutchins?"

"I got it out of a local cop who's been in touch with Darnell."

Stanley Schaulton considered these words. He asked, "You got any specifics?"

"Yes," said the pathologist who then read off the directions to Dennysville and the names of the back roads to take to Dr. Jeremy Chess' fishing camp.

Dante Callanti sauntered through the terminal building carrying no luggage. He came up to the Hertz counter and rented a Mercury with a false driver's license and cash. After signing the papers and snatching up the keys, Callanti asked the clerk casually, "You have a package here for Mr. Tom Engels? I'm supposed to pick it up for him."

"Yes, Mr. Campbell," said the wizened old man. "I do." He reached under the counter and hoisted up a small canvas suitcase.

Callanti took it and walked towards the parking lot. He found the blue sedan whose plates matched the numbers on his key ring, unlocked the door and flipped the suitcase onto the front seat. Getting behind the wheel, he spent several minutes adjusting the position of the seat and the mirrors, then turned on the engine.

Backing out, Callanti thought, *I'm damned glad I sent that little prick, Pizzi, back to Miami. I like it a hell of a lot better working alone.*

Like the old days.

Ike took Judy to see a new Harrison Ford film at a local movie theater, then out to dinner at a sea-side restaurant with great atmosphere and even better sea food. They polished off two bottles of a very dry Liebfraumilch, then drove back along the highway to the Grand-View Motel at the water's edge on the outskirts of St. Andrews.

Ike switched off the ignition and the lights and took Judy's hands in his. "You know," he said, "there must be something to this fate thing. Just think of the probability of you and me being here together tonight. A year ago I was an overworked, happily married Philadelphia neurosurgeon with two beautiful daughters. Then, six shots later, I was a lost man. I stopped working and stopped living, then answered the craziest ad I've ever seen—out of pure boredom—and got mixed up in something I don't comprehend at all, except that I understand perfectly that I'm falling head over heels in love with you and am ecstatic to be here at this moment."

Judy slumped her head onto his shoulder. "Ike, one year ago, my whole world was my practice and my research and Yale. Three days ago I met you. I don't understand anything." She inched over and kissed him deeply.

"Inside," he said.

Judy stepped out of the passenger door. She looked out across the bay, then down the long stretch of highway, eerily illuminated in the bright moonlight. She slammed her door and the little bulb inside flicked off. She turned towards Ike and dimly saw the sharp contours of his handsome face. Suddenly they were brightened by the high beams of an automobile off in the distance, one which approached them slowly from the north and east.

Ike fished the room key out of his pocket and inserted it into the lock. He took her by the hand and they slipped as one into the dark room.

Dante Callanti drove with deliberateness, his eyes searching for a red Porche and two blacks. He passed the sign indicating the St. Andrews town line and slowed down. A quarter mile ahead he spotted the bright neon sign: **GRAND-VIEW MOTEL** and underneath: **VACANCY**.

Though the distance was great he thought he saw two people—a man and a woman—standing next to a parked vehicle. Was it red? A Porche? Were they black? He didn't know. His heart quickened.

He pulled to a stop on the shoulder two hundred yards from the Grand-View, then unzipped the canvas suitcase. He had examined its contents briefly at a gas station back in Fredericton and had admired the .25 caliber, silencer-equipped Beretta which now rested in his breast pocket. He knew that, amongst other things, the suitcase contained a pair of high-powered binoculars.

Raising the lenses to his eyes, Callanti was twisting the focus knobs when a strident beeping startled him. He allowed the binoculars to fall into his lap. The beeping came from an inside pouch in the suitcase. He flicked on his flashlight and trained the beam in the direction of the sound. He lifted the tele-pager out of the pouch, surprised he had not noticed it before.

Embossed on the black plastic was a phone number.

Dante Callanti screeched to a stop in front of Jed's Diner, fifty yards from the Grand-View Motel. He slipped into the antique oak phone booth and dialed. An operator told him to call Tom Engels immediately, that it was an emergency.

Callanti called Stanley Schaulton in Dallas.

He was several miles past St. Andrews, en route

to the international bridge at St. Stephens, when he had a vague mental image of the distant car in the Grand-View parking lot and the two people who stood in shadow next to it. The image left his mind.

Callanti paid the toll and crossed into Calais, Maine.

The image returned.

Unlikely, he thought, now anticipating delivering bullets to two suckers' brains in the dark of the night amidst the silence of the wilderness.

The Cue Ball snatched off his toupee and caressed his bald pate lovingly.

It would be more exciting this way.

CHAPTER 13

9 *May*

FBI Agent Jack Galvin leaned on a boulder at the beginning of the unmarked, unnamed dirt road which led to the cabin where Ike and Judy had been staying. It was three-thirty in the morning. Galvin, a mid-thirties, dark-haired, homely fellow, surveyed the entire road with his infrared night scope.

The miniature speaker attached to his left ear crackled, then he heard, "Suspicious human approaching on foot slowly. Should be in your view in about a minute."

Galvin passed the message along to the seven men posted at thirty yard intervals around the cabin, then peered intently into his scope. Forty seconds later he spotted the distinctive shape of a man walking stealthily towards him. He held his breath as the man passed within four yards then continued on to the camp.

Dante Callanti, Beretta in hand, moved with feline grace. Twenty yards from the front porch of the tiny dwelling, he stopped and listened, hearing initially the chirping and clicking of myriad insects, the rustling of small mammals and frogs in the underbrush and the distant knocking from the river of a beaver's teeth on wood. Pausing, he shone his flashlight on the wooden structure and the clearing in front of it. *No car*, he thought. *They're probably not back from wherever they went. I'll slip inside and wait.*

Callanti was lifting his right foot to take a first step when he heard a distinctively human sound — a fart. His heart racing, he directed his flashlight all about him, scanning the dense woods for the provenance of that ominous noise. Callanti saw nothing unusual.

He calmed himself. *It could've been a deer or something — maybe a bear. They must fart all the time. I just never heard it.* He advanced on the cabin. *No,* he concluded, *a goddamned person just fucking ripped one!* Callanti raced onto the porch and tried the door. It opened.

Inside, he slowed his breathing and listened, finally relieved that no one was present. He switched off his light. Crawling behind a tattered couch he looked through a screened window, certain that someone was out there.

Jack Galvin pressed the button of the radio transmitter suspended from his belt.

Dante Callanti heard a new noise—a hissing. He kept his gaze fixed on the moonlit clearing. He became light-headed and a bit dizzy. His vision blurred. He moved his body clumsily towards the hissing, but never reached the canister of surgical anesthetic.

Callanti slumped to the wooden floor unconscious.

The morning sky was bright and blue, the sun a sizzling casaba on the eastern horizon. Ike whistled "Down The Field," leading Judy, a bounce in his step, from their room to Jed's Diner. After a huge breakfast he telephoned Hollister, who advised him of the capture of their stalker.

"Ike," said the detective, "I'm telling you it's oh-fucking-kay for you to go back to camp, get your stuff and return to civilization. They got this asshole under lock and key this very moment in Bangor. They'll be flying him here this afternoon for arraignment for the murder of that Trooper. He literally walked right the fuck into their trap."

"All right, Captain. I believe you. Judy and I'll

be going back to New Haven to continue her experiments on the 'PG' extracts. How's Sophie?"

"Much better. She's going to be transferred to Ogdensburg today. As soon as she's able I'm going to ask her to finger this dirtball for her assault. Ike, this guy's a fucking animal—he beat the living shit out of an old lady, then stuffed her into a dryer."

"What's his name?"

"The FBI has no idea. They found twelve pieces of identification on his person—each with a different name. They're certain he's never been booked before. But, Ike, they're shitting in their pants; they reprinted this jerk-off—he's definitely the fucking Cue Ball. He's the lowest form of scum."

"Any idea why he was after me and whom he was working for?"

"Nope. He hasn't talked—hasn't uttered a single fucking word. You know, like a deaf guy."

"I'll call you from New Haven," said Ike Darnell. "Bye."

Ike returned to his table with a smile.

He picked up his coffee cup, took a sip and told Judy, "They nabbed the guy who was after us. What do you say we head back to New Haven? If you'll have me, I'd like to give you a hand with your experiments."

"I see. So it's back to the Yankee Carriage House," she said in jest.

"Not exactly. There's this real nice lady who

lives in this fancy penthouse. I'd sort of like to stay with her. Do you think that could be arranged?"

Judy Frymoyer nodded and took his huge hands in hers.

Stanley Schaulton placed three phone calls between one and one-thirty PM.

The first was to an attorney in Bangor, Maine.

Next he called Miami, Florida and spoke with a man by the name of Frankie Pizzaro.

Lastly, he called Harold Hutchins in Syracuse.

There were no windows in Dr. Frymoyer's animal room. Accordingly, when Alice Hyde opened the door from the main lab, she frequently was greeted by the eerie red glows from multiple monkey eyes, as the room light was reflected from them. She knew this was the so-called "red reflex," made possible by light passing through a normal lens, striking the blood-rich retina, then bouncing back toward the viewer. On this afternoon Alice thought there was a subtle difference in what she saw. Several of the eyes were dulled and dim.

She turned on the overhead fluorescent lights and looked carefully at one of the Rhesus monkeys. Pulling a small penlight from her pocket, she shone it obliquely at the monkey's face, revealing an unequivocal milky-looking film in the center of the eyeball. She discovered the same finding in two others.

Alice noted these findings in the ledger, administered the injections of "PG" extract, then walked to the hospital clinical laboratory to obtain the reports of the blood analyses she had submitted earlier.

Attorney William Eakins entered the FBI Field Office in Bangor and walked up to the desk. "Excuse me," he said to the man on duty. "I'm the assigned counsel for the guy you're extraditing to New York, a fellow by the name of . . . " He glanced at a paper he had pulled from his pocket. "Campbell. William Campbell."

"Your name?"

Eakins identified himself, then was led to the holding room where Dante Callanti sat silently.

"May I be alone with my client?" the attorney asked the agent guarding him.

"Sure. Just a minute." He undid the prisoner's handcuffs and reattached them to a metal ring embedded in the cinder block wall. "Be my guest. Just knock on that door when you're done."

Eakins sat across the table from his client. He extracted a notepad from his pocket, wrote *Schaulton* on the blank paper, then showed it to Dante Callanti who nodded.

"Cigarette?" asked Eakins, producing a package

of Marlboros and a lighter. He saw Callanti smile. "Keep the pack," Eakins said, pushing it to him.

Callanti lighted a cigarette with his free hand.

"I've examined the extradition documentation, Mr. Campbell," said Eakins, certain that the room was bugged, "and I'm afraid the government has shown good cause. There's nothing I or anyone else can do to prevent it. They found your prints on a vehicle from which a man killed a New York State Trooper. Any questions?"

Callanti shook his head.

Eakins wrote: *DON'T WORRY!*, then left the room.

The transport of a patient from one EconoMed Clinic to another was handled by a fleet of in-house ambulances. Before each ambulance left, the Emergency Medical Technician who rode in back with the patient checked out an emergency drug case—actually a huge tackle box filled with vials and syringes—from the nursing superintendent in the out-patient department.

Dr. Harold Hutchins left his office carrying a small package, about the size of a pound of butter, which was wrapped in plain brown paper. Having seen to it that the head nurse was summoned elsewhere and having determined precisely which ambulance would transport Sophie Lepert to Ogdensburg, Hutchins entered the empty nursing office with confidence. He opened the tackle box on the desk and inserted his package into its bottom, below several pairs of sterile gloves and two bags of intravenous fluids.

Returning to his office, Hutchins called Stanley Schaulton. "It's done," he said.

Frankie Pizzaro, known to his intimates as "Pizzi," was a short, neckless, powerfully built man of forty who was far better and far more comfortable with his fists and feet, than with firearms. He waited patiently near a telephone booth at Hancock Airport in Syracuse.

The phone rang.

Pizzaro wrote down the markings he would be looking for on the ambulance and the plate number.

He walked quickly to his rented Chevrolet and soon was out in traffic. Pizzaro parked at the rest area just north of Exit 30 on I-81 and, through high-powered binoculars, watched the vehicles whiz by him.

Ike stopped Judy's Porche in her designated spot in the underground garage, then followed her up to her apartment. After a quick meal and a shower, they walked the two blocks to Judy's lab. It was five PM.

Judy entered the lab with a sense of anticipation, of excitement. She had called from Maine and had been advised of Alice Hyde's preliminary findings.

Judy encountered Alice in the animal room, in the process of administering the last injections for the day. "How's it coming?"

Alice glanced over her shoulder at her boss, then back at the squirming monkey she was trying to inject. "Fine, Dr. Frymoyer. Did you—" She stopped in mid-sentence upon seeing Ike.

"It's OK, Alice. This is Dr. Darnell from Philadelphia. He'll be assisting me with these experiments."

Alice nodded to Ike and continued, "Did you give any thought to what I told you?"

"Yes. Where is the data?"

"Top drawer."

Judy removed a sheaf of papers and examined them. "Ike," she said ebulliently, "look at this!" Ike came to her side. "Six animals from the PG-1 group and four from the other are producing low to moderate levels of an abnormal immunoglobulin—the same monoclonal protein!"

"Judy," Ike protested, "I know how to excise brain tumors and repair herniated discs and I did do well in medical school, but I do not understand what you're saying. Pretend I'm a moron and go slow."

"OK," she said with a broad smile, delighted to

have a leg up on this masterful man, "In the bloodstream there are three types of formed elements: red cells, platelets and white cells. There are two classes of white cells: the leukocytes and the lymphocytes. Are you with me so far?"

Ike nodded.

"There are two kinds of lymphocytes: B-cells and T-cells. The B-cells make antibodies. Am I too quick for you, Doctor?"

"No. You're just right," said Ike.

"All right," continued Judy. "Some of these monkeys' B-cells are making abnormal antibodies, presumably as a result of our injecting increasing amounts of PG into them. PG, therefore, must be an antigen—a protein which elicits such a response."

"I'm with you. What is the significance of these antibodies?"

"That, Ike, is precisely what we must determine."

"How?"

"Clinically, by blood testing, by biopsy, by autopsy—by whatever means necessary."

"Dr. Frymoyer," interrupted Alice, "I made an unusual observation this morning. It appears to me that some of these animals, in fact, some of the same ones who are making that antibody, are developing cataracts."

Galvanized, Judy stood up. "Show me!" she commanded.

Fifteen minutes later, with the assistance of an ophthalmoscope, Judy and Ike confirmed Alice Hyde's suspicions.

Returning with Ike to her consultation room, Judy rippled with intellectual passion. She closed the door and spun toward him. "Ike, Natalie Lepert and Peter Tillers were killed because they learned that Stiles Laboratory's house dust extract contained an antigen which stimulated synthesis of a killer protein."

"Killer protein? Are you sure?"

"Of course, I'm not sure! But that's what I strongly suspect. I believe that somehow some scientist at Stiles stumbled upon how to tell the immune system to promote premature aging. It's been theorized by immunologists for years that aging is an immune system task. There's even a very rare disease called progyria which causes five and six year olds to die of old age. There's one thing, however, that's not at all clear to me."

"What's that?"

"If that's what they're actually doing—why? Why, Ike, would anyone want people to get older faster? It makes no sense." She paused. Her eyes flashed. "Did David Lepert have cataracts?"

"I don't know. We can easily call his family doctor in Ogdensburg."

"Call him right now, Ike," said Dr. Judy Frymoyer.

Ten minutes later, having learned of Harvey Martin's untimely death, Ike set the phone down. "Sophie would know. Let's try to contact her."

Frankie Pizzaro spotted the ambulance as it descended the small knoll south of the rest area. He brought his binoculars up and confirmed the plate number, then switched on his engine and pulled into traffic.

Two miles north and fifty yards behind the ambulance, Pizzaro pressed the button of the radio transmitter in his hand.

The white and red emergency vehicle erupted in a mammoth fireball.

Pizzaro got off at the next exit, crossed under the highway, then headed south to New Haven.

Stanley Schaulton stopped his kelly green Mercedes at the rear entrance of EconoMed Tower in central Dallas. He entered the security code on the keypad and the doors opened with a muted hiss. Schaulton took the elevator to the thirty-seventh floor and strode into the conference room.

As he took his seat at the head of the table, Schaulton felt uneasy about this emergency board meeting he had called. He was concerned that these pompous and, in some cases, very stupid men would fail to comprehend the truth if he told it.

Should he reveal all?

The only other person, besides Harold Hutchins, who had known the significance of the additive—its discoverer—was embedded in forty tons of concrete in a bridge abutment near Fort Worth. He, Stanley Schaulton, had learned how to synthesize and purify it, had set up an independent lab whose sole function it was to produce it—but that lab, albeit another EconoMed subsidiary, had no concept as to how their product was used.

For years Schaulton had gloated over the fact that this extraordinary substance had been responsible for EconoMed International's meteoric rise in the health care industry and had made him personally a multi-billionaire. He thought it the greatest and shrewdest maneuver in the history of world business. In order to preserve its income potential, Schaulton knew that he must eliminate that meddling Sophie Lepert, Ike Darnell and now Judy Frymoyer.

Finally he concluded that it would be imprudent to make full disclosure to his board. A limited hang-out would have to suffice.

"Gentlemen," he began, "an informant of mine at the FDA has just advised me that some of the products made by one of our subsidiaries, Stiles

Labs, may be contaminated by potentially harmful substances. Accordingly, I called this meeting to obtain a vote for voluntary closure of Stiles, pending full in-house investigation."

"But Stiles," said a well-tanned septuagenarian investment banker on Schaulton's right, "does an annual gross of eight hundred and forty million. Why don't we wait till the Feds force us to act. That's not exactly pocket change."

"True, Edmund, but Stiles' take is only two per cent of EconoMed's total annual income. If the Feds prove their allegations, we're looking at astronomical legal fees and a hell of a lot of real bad press. On balance, we've much to lose. With respect to the bottom line, we'll do better with voluntary withdrawal.

"Just what are these so-called harmful substances?" asked a steel magnate with a Ph.D. in biochemistry.

"Don't know. Their complaint won't be in our hands for at least a month."

"Listen, gentlemen," interjected the retired Federal Court Judge responsible for the numerous government contracts which had, during EconoMed's embryonic years, catapulted it to national prominence, "Stanley's right. It's the bottom line that's important. I move the question."

Stanley Schaulton's proposal passed without further debate.

Handcuffed to FBI Agent Jack Galvin, Dante Callanti sipped his 7-Up and smoked Marlboro after Marlboro. Although he had seen the Bangor attorney remove the cellophane from the package, he was certain that some of the filter tips were a bit soggy. *Must be an old pack*, he thought.

The Pan-Am jet banked slowly and began its descent into Syracuse. Callanti saw the "No Smoking" light flash on and extinguished one of the slightly soggy cigarettes.

It was as he was walking through the Hancock Airport terminal that Callanti felt the first semblance of a headache and a strange chill which emanated from the core of his body.

By the time he arrived at the police station, he was certain he was coming down with the flu.

"Listen, I've got tonight and tomorrow off," said Detective Captain Bertram Hollister. "If you think you're able, why don't you let me run you to Ogdensburg?"

Sophie Lepert sat up in her hospital bed. "That sounds terrific. I guess it was lucky for me that there was a critically ill newborn in Alexandria Bay and that the hospital's helicopter wasn't functional."

"Yep," said Hollister, "they had to take their isolette with them and didn't have room for a patient. I'll be back in a minute, Mrs. Lepert," said

Hollister arising. "I'll hunt up your doctor and see if he'll release you."

Near midnight, in the darkness of the unlit room, one of the monkeys in the PG-1 group awakened from sleep clutching its left chest.

It was short of breath, nauseated and sweating.

CHAPTER 14

10 May

Judy Frymoyer stretched the carcass of the dead monkey across her dissecting table and switched on the high intensity lamp. Though puzzled by the death of the animal, she was relieved that Ike had significant expertise in surgical pathology and could perform a meaningful autopsy. All business, she watched him make the opening incision.

Thirty minutes later Ike had dissected out the vital organs from the chest and abdomen and laid them on the empty instrument table. "Before we take the brain," he said, "let's see what we've got here."

Judy had observed that the monkey's lungs and liver were congested; she suspected a cardiac death. She eyed Ike's first cut into the heart and saw the discolored muscle, indicative of acute myocardial infarction.

"It appears that he had a heart attack," said Ike. "A massive one. I don't think we need look any further for a cause of death."

"A heart attack in a two year old monkey?" queried Judy. "Why?"

Ike passed his fingers over the left coronary artery. "Here's why. This vessel is hard as a rock." He transected it with his scalpel and inspected the cut ends. "Atherosclerosis, Judy. Really advanced."

"All right, I've seen enough. My suspicions are correct. PG triggers the synthesis of an antibody, which—and I am sure the microscopic picture will verify this—causes rapid aging of various target organs. Ike, let's get these tissues into formalin and send them down to pathology for processing. It'll take them twenty-four hours to make slides."

"Sure, but let's not forget the brain. Remember, that was one of David Lepert's chief problems." He lifted the power saw and cut off the top of the skull. Removing the brain, he commented, "It's shriveled—just like in Alzheimer's."

Back in her private office Judy paced nervously. Ike sat and watched her. "I know what you're thinking," he said.

"Do you?"

"Yes, you're wondering what we should do with this extraordinary information. I've been mulling it over, too."

Judy sat behind her desk, hands crossed and

scratching their opposite upper arms. Ike had been correct about her thoughts. "The government. Let's take it right to the FDA. Stiles Labs is the biggest supplier of allergenic extracts in the world. Three refrigerators in my office are filled with their products."

"I noticed that," said Ike pensively. "And that, my dear, is the problem."

"I don't follow."

"You've been administering Stiles' house dust extract to your many patients for years. Right?"

"Sure. And so have thousands of my colleagues."

"That's my point. Have you ever noticed or has any other allergist ever reported premature aging in any of his patients?"

Judy considered this question. "Of course not. All right, Dr. Smarts, I see what you're driving at. For some reason or other, this PG was added selectively to certain allergy treatment sets."

"Exactly! That's why Marvin Hambly found there was a difference between what he submitted for processing and what Natalie Lepert gave him in the form of her father's serum."

"But, Ike, as we've seen, that's murder."

"I don't think that was the objective. Do you believe that a healthy Rhesus monkey—or a human being—would die quickly, if it were given tiny doses of this stuff at weekly, biweekly or monthly intervals?"

"You're right. I did push the dose to the maximum. No, the slow administration of this antigen would probably cause a series of indolent, progressive chronic diseases. But, I come back to why—it just doesn't make any sense."

Ike was silent.

"Do you think it was a whacko?" asked Judy. "You know, like the cyanide in the Tylenol. A psychopathic random killer, only on slow speed."

"Unlikely. My gut feeling is that Natalie Lepert was murdered in a very clever, very shrewd and calculating fashion—not the work of a screwball. She was killed because she'd discovered PG—and the reason she came across it was that it had been used on her father."

Judy stood and continued her pacing. "What, then, do we do?"

"Contact the man who is most likely to know why."

Puzzled, Judy looked at Ike, then heard him say, "I say we call Stanley Schaulton."

Frankie Pizzaro had already planned the double execution. In his mind it was simple. He'd walk into the lab as soon as the young white girl left and deliver rapid killing blows to the necks of the two black doctors. He knew he'd have to give some sort of cover story to lull them into complacency, so he'd already removed the *Miami Herald* press passes and ID from his baggage and put them into his jacket pocket. Although he knew he didn't look like a newspaper reporter, he was certain the ruse would at least gain him entry—and that would be good enough.

Pizzaro continued to wait in the lobby of the Sterling Hall of Medicine, aware (from his previous visit to New Haven with Dante Callanti) that the lab tech always exited that way. He continued to stare without comprehension at the first page of the second section of *The Wall Street Journal* and nodded politely at a passing Oriental in a white coat who said "Herro" to him.

Pizzaro glanced at his watch. It was 10:30 AM. She'd be leaving for lunch in about an hour.

Bertram Hollister had awakened in Sophie Lepert's guest room at dawn, then had breakfasted and gone to visit Sophie once again at the Ogdensburg EconoMed Clinic before returning to Syracuse. During that visit, Sophie had mentioned Ike Darnell's brief search for her daughter's computer records and had told him of the fireproof box, their inability to find it in the attic and the totally erased hard disk. Absently, while drifting off into a Demerol daze, she had suggested looking through her husband's papers stored above the carriage house.

Now Hollister climbed the rickety, steep steps and emerged into a huge, single, high-ceilinged room about the size of a basketball court. He spotted the brown cardboard file boxes on the far wall.

Flicking on the overhead light, he pulled a box from the top of the pile and began to sift through it.

Stanley Schaulton had slept little last night. He was, above all else, a shrewd and cunning businessman. He had spent his entire adult life calculating angles and edges and had used the stock market to convert a few thousand dollars into billions. During the night his thinking had changed. He now felt, deep within his bones, that the *right* move was not to cover up the existence of the additive, eliminate the meddlers, then resume his astonishingly profitable control of EconoMed International. Rather, he was certain that his most prudent course would be to dump his stock, resign as CEO, pump everything into his Zurich account and laugh his ass off on his way to a European vacation.

So decided, he faced several problems. First, there was Harold Hutchins. He had selected Hutchins to oversee the additive pilot project in upstate New York. Once it had proved successful, Schaulton had implemented it, with Hutchins' assistance (as a *quid pro quo* for a cut of the profits) clandestinely at every EconoMed Clinic in the country. Hutchins, therefore, represented a definite obstacle.

Second, there was SAS Commodities, Inc., the tiny laboratory in Ardmore, Pennsylvania which manufactured the additive, amino acid by amino acid, utilizing the most sophisticated protein biosynthetic tools known to man. Schaulton had not, of course, apprised the scientists at SAS of the commercial use of their product. He'd paid them well to ask no questions.

Third, there was Melvin Hinkle, the Wharton-trained accountant who picked up the vials from SAS on a weekly basis and transported them personally to specific Stiles distributors around the country at Schaulton's direction. For ten thousand dollars a week, Hinkle had been savvy enough to do his job without one iota of curiosity.

Schaulton's fourth problem he regarded as his greatest. If the CEO of a major corporation suddenly sells off millions of shares of a blue chip stock trading at its all time high, then he is virtually requesting an SEC investigation regarding insider trading. How to accomplish this task had consumed his sleepless night.

Schaulton sipped his scotch and water slowly, his mind churning. The stock solution came to him in a flash of brilliance. Dr. Leonard Woodley.

Woodley, a member of Schaulton's regular golf

foursome had impregnated his office nurse five years ago and had commiserated his plight to Schaulton over drinks in the clubhouse one sunny afternoon. The nurse, he had told Schaulton, was threatening to blackmail him to his wife. Though a wealthy cardiologist, Woodley had seven children, each approaching college age. *What can I do, Stan? The bitch is going to bleed me—and those Ivy League schools aren't cheap.* Schaulton had told him not to worry and had resolved the matter definitively.

Schaulton called Dr. Woodley.

Though in the middle of seeing patients, he left his office immediately after Schaulton's summons and arrived at the mansion in ten minutes.

"Drink, Lennie?" asked Stanley Schaulton.

The cardiologist swallowed hard and nodded. He sat across from Schaulton and downed it in a gulp. "What can I do for you, Stan?"

"I need to have a non-lethal heart attack."

"Excuse me?"

"Lennie," he said in measured tones, "you will prepare a report, complete with substantiating electrocardiograms, indicating that, because of significant cardiac damage, you have recommended that I stop gainful employment, liquidate my assets and retire. Do I make myself clear?"

Shocked and bewildered, Woodley sputtered, "Stan, that would be impossible. A given patient's ECG is as unique as a fingerprint. If it is faked, then compared with an old one, the ruse would be obvious."

Schaulton sipped his scotch and smiled. "Lennie, my boy, just think how bad you'd feel if I stopped making monthly contributions to Linda Hagel's checking account—or even worse, gave your wife her new address in Indiana. Your boy's a junior at Harvard, isn't he?"

The doctor's eyes were wide, the back of his shirt soaked and stuck to his cashmere jacket. "Sophomore, actually."

" 'Twould be a damn shame if the boy couldn't finish, now wouldn't it? And how about young Lisa? Smith, isn't it?"

"When do you need the report, Stan?"

"This afternoon."

"It will be no problem."

"Fine, Lennie. Fine. You may go now."

After Woodley had left, Schaulton picked up his phone and called an old hunting buddy of his, Jeffrey Palmer, at the Dean's Office of the Yale School of Medicine. "Jeff, it's Stan. There's a business associate of mine who I believe is, at this very moment, waiting in the lobby of your building. I should be most appreciative if you would hop down there and ask him to call me at once. It's an urgent matter."

"Sure, Stan, sure," said Dean Palmer, flattered

to be contacted by his old friend and a generous contributor to Yale's many research programs.

Alice Hyde left Dr. Frymoyer's lab and, taking the steps, walked into the lobby and towards the front door. She paid no regard to the short, muscle-bound man sitting on the couch, though she spied the Dean approach him and greet him warmly.

Hoisting her tote bag high on her shoulder, Alice gave no further attention to the man, exited into the sunshine and strolled leisurely to Pepe's Luncheonette.

"Pizzi," said Stanley Schaulton into the phone, "your plans have changed. Listen carefully."

"Sure, boss. Shoot."

Unable to reach Captain Hollister in Syracuse, Ike Darnell set down the phone. Before calling EconoMed's main man, Ike had thought it wise to discuss his intentions with the detective. After his initial decision to call Schaulton, Ike had become unsure of the ramifications of such a bold move.

"Hollister won't be available until this evening," he told an anxious Judy Frymoyer. "It's worth the wait. Anyhow, what's the rush?"

"True. Let's go back to the apartment and grab a bite."

"Is that all?" asked Ike, pouting.

"No," said Judy, a twinkle in her eye. "That's not all."

Five minutes after returning to his office, Bertram Hollister learned of the extradited prisoner's inexplicable death that morning at University Hospital from a particularly virulent form of meningococcal meningitis, and the violent deaths of the two EMT's in the ambulance that would have been transporting Sophie Lepert.

He placed the four diskettes he had found in the box in Sophie Lepert's carriage house into his safe. As he was nearly computer-illiterate, he'd decided to try to examine them later.

Exhausted, Hollister poured himself some coffee and lighted a Camel. He began to sort through the fragments of information which had come to his attention during the past several days, many of which he felt were related to the death of Dr. Natalie Lepert. His thoughts went round and round. He stubbed out his cigarette and torched another. One name kept popping up: Harold Hutchins.

Hutchins had worked with Natalie. Now Hollister knew he had been screwing her. He'd autopsied her. He probably killed her. But how? And why? That was what bothered the detective the most—his inability to perceive a possible motive. *Does it have something to do with this fucking PG crap that Ike's gone hog-wild about? But, if so, why? Why would a class act like Hutchins, a doctor, a wealthy guy, a big shot at a prestigious place like EconoMed, knock off another physician? For some fucking protein?*

Hollister knew that his leak to Hutchins had brought The Cue Ball into the FBI trap. Did Hutchins contact the man directly? Is there somebody higher who's been pulling both their strings? Could it possibly be Stanley Schaulton, one of the richest men in the world?

The puzzle pieces failed to come together.

He picked up his telephone and dialed a number. "I'd like to speak to Dr. Hutchins," he said to the receptionist.

Moments later: "This is Dr. Hutchins."

"Hutchins, it's Captain Hollister. I'd like to meet with you."

Hollister heard a pause, then: "Why?"

"I want to speak with you about Natalie Lepert's death."

"Damnit, Hollister. What's there to discuss?"

"A protein added to a house dust extract," said the detective. He paused and waited. Hutchins did not respond. "You there, Doctor?"

"I'm here."

"What do you know about this protein?"

"Nothing. There must be hundreds of proteins in house dust. Why should I know or care?"

Hollister was silent. He listened to the pathologist's rapid breathing and knew what it meant. "I'll be at Rusty's in an hour, Doctor. Why not stop in and have a drink with me? I'll tell you everything I know." The detective set the phone down in the cradle without waiting for a response.

Stanley Schaulton picked his way through the Dallas rush hour traffic. He'd spent the past hour and a half with his personal attorney, Hiram Folger, whom, like Leonard Woodley, he had in his pocket. That the lawyer would never talk Schaulton was sure. He'd given him Woodley's report, his letter of resignation and twelve pages of specific instructions regarding liquidation of his EconoMed shares, including the number of his Swiss bank account and the various phone numbers and post office boxes where he could be reached during his "convalescence."

Returning to his lavish home, Schaulton stopped at the adjacent air strip to supervise the loading of his personal effects onto his private Lear jet.

Schaulton was relying on a brutal Italian by the name of Pizzi to take care of his importunate obstacles.

Schaulton entered his study and made one last call to Dr. Jessica Pahler in Chicago. He told her the code word Pizzi would use in order to be paid for his work, warning her that Pizzi had lethal hands and feet. "No problem," said the psychopathic pharmacologist. "My accuracy with this dart gun at up to fifteen feet is a hundred per cent. Would you prefer botulinus toxin, straight cyanide or succinyl choline?"

"Which is quickest?"

"The succinyl choline. It will be a matter of seconds."

"Good," said Schaulton. "Then I want his body put through a meat grinder and fed to dogs."

"As you wish."

Stanley Schaulton hung up. He did not care one whit what Ike Darnell, Judy Frymoyer or Sophie Lepert could uncover about the additive and its relationship to Natalie Lepert's death. In less than forty-eight hours it would not be possible for such news to hurt him.

EconoMed International would take the fall— and he wouldn't own a single share.

Schaulton smiled broadly. He would be squeaky clean in London or Paris, free to seduce any pretty young woman he could find. The thought warmed his heart and gave him a hard-on.

His first reaction was to phone Schaulton immediately after Hollister's call, but Harold Hutchins judged it prudent to meet with the detective first to feel him out. He left his office and hopped into the elevator. Though he'd initially pressed the

"L" button, he decided, after passing the fourth floor, to stop in the mezzanine mail room to check his box. Hutchins exited onto the lavish landing outside of the in-house postal service. From his mail slot he could see down into the main lobby through the ornate balcony.

He flipped through several bills and professional letters and was reinserting them into the box, when his casual glance transmuted into a fixed stare.

Harold Hutchins' heart raced. Sweat poured from his armpits and forehead. He pushed his glasses up a bit on his nose, hoping that it was a mistaken image.

But it wasn't.

He saw, waiting patiently for the up elevator, a man he'd hoped never to see again in his life—certainly not in his own building. Hutchins didn't know the man's name, just that he was one of Stanley Schaulton's hired killers. He squinted as the man entered the elevator, then watched him raise his hand to the panel of buttons.

Harold Hutchins became faint and nauseated.

He'd seen the man press "11"—his floor!

Hutchins raced down the fire stairs and out into the rear courtyard of the clinic, near the emergency ambulance entrance. He spotted a taxi, ran to it, got in and ordered the driver to take him to Rusty's on Warren Street.

Entering the Yuppie bar, the pathologist headed straight for the rear and ducked into a phone booth. He removed an address book from his breast pocket, then dialed the number which, owing to his direct link, he'd never had to use.

"Yes?" he heard through the wire.

"Schaulton, what the hell are you trying to pull?"

"And who might this be?"

"Harold Hutchins. Why did you send your goon to my office?"

"Hutchins, what in God's name are you talking about?" asked Schaulton with an air of innocence.

"I'm talking about the short greaseball who always worked with that guy who died this morning from meningitis. I saw him coming toward my office."

"Where are you now, Harold? I believe there's been a misunderstanding. There *has* been a change of plans. I'd like to fly to Syracuse this evening to discuss it with you."

Hutchins remembered the macabre scene he'd witnessed in Room 1342 of Harah's Casino and Hotel in Atlantic City last July, of what had happened to the three men representing the syndicate hoping to buy control of EconoMed. He saw smashed faces, actually squished flat by a blunt instrument. Later, Schaulton had told him that the damage had been inflicted by a man's hand. Hutchins recalled whom Schaulton had dispatched to that job.

He was terrified.

Losing the grip of the phone in his sweaty hand, he dropped it. He watched it bounce, tethered by the black wire, until it stopped. Hutchins thought he was witnessing his own death. He grabbed the receiver. "OK, I'll meet you. When and where?"

"Gate Twenty-two." Schaulton glanced at his watch. "Eight-thirty, your time."

"I'll be there," said Harold Hutchins, hanging up, not allowing a reply.

Bertram Hollister was just arising from his desk chair and about to go out the door when his intercom buzzed. Tightening the knot in his tie, he snatched up the phone.

It was Ike Darnell.

"Ike! How the fuck are you?"

"Captain," said Ike, "we've got to talk. Judy and I believe we know why Natalie Lepert was killed."

"The fucking protein? Right?"

"Correct. It's the protein, all right, but the astounding thing is what its biological properties are."

"Don't get uppity with me, Doctor. I don't understand that shit."

"You'll understand this—PG causes laboratory

monkeys to age rapidly. They're developing cataracts, heart attacks and shriveled brains. We know that Natalie brought the protein to Judy's former colleague—the one who was killed—in order to do the same experiments we're doing right now. There's no question in my mind she was killed because of it. The key men are Stanley Schaulton and Harold Hutchins."

Hollister had lighted a new Camel. He sat back puffing. "Why, Ike? What the fuck good is it to get people older faster?"

"I don't know that, Captain—but it was important enough to somebody to kill Dr. Lepert."

Hollister tried to comprehend what he was hearing. *What the fuck is going on here?* he thought. "Ike, we've got to meet. Can you come to Syracuse?"

"When?"

"Tonight?"

Hollister heard a muted conversation in the background, then: "I don't think so. We've got too much to do here."

"Damnit, Ike! I'm going to be meeting with Hutchins in twenty minutes. If I can convince him that you've really got something, he might sing to save his own skin."

"Call me after your meeting." Ike gave Hollister Judy's lab number and hung up.

The detective left his office, got behind the

wheel of his unmarked car and drove into the heavy traffic.

In the cabin of the Lear jet Stanley Schaulton nursed a scotch and soda. He peered out the window at Pittsburgh, Pennsylvania, his eyes now sunken deep into his skull. *It's going all wrong*, he thought. *How could Pizzi be so sloppy as to be seen by his target? If Hutchins is not eliminated promptly, and he talks, then I am in some very deep stuff.*

Mellowed by the alcohol, Schaulton recalled his boyhood days in Lubbock, Texas. He remembered being dirt poor, hungry, filthy, sometimes not having a home or a bed, sleeping in abandoned cars with his parents and his brother, being abused by vagrant hoboes. Then he'd raised a stake at seventeen, lost it in an oil scam at eighteen, raised it again. By twenty he was a millionaire, many times over. He'd never looked back, had changed his name, his appearance. *And now because of some sloppy thug, I might lose it all. If Hutchins talks to the authorities, the SEC'll be on my back in ten seconds. They'll know why EconoMed was so successful and why I got out. Damn, it'll make Boesky look like a Little Leaguer. I've got to silence that son of a bitch.*

The speaker in the cabin crackled to life. He heard his pilot say, "Mr. Schaulton, you have an urgent call on the scrambled line."

Schaulton rushed to the cockpit. "Who is it, Freddie?"

"A man. Wouldn't identify himself. Obviously, he knows how to reach you."

Schaulton nodded, then maneuvered on rubbery legs to the private compartment at the rear of the plane and lifted the receiver of the red telephone. "Yes?"

"It's me, boss. I can't locate the pretty boy. His office girl says he left a coupla minutes before I got there."

"GODDAMNIT, FRANKIE! You've really screwed this up!" Schaulton realized he was getting too overtly excited, a bad move when dealing with a scumball like Frankie Pizzaro. He tried to calm himself, but kept feeling the tethers of poverty and depravity pulling him into the past. He realized how much he hated what he'd been. Finally, he asked, "How about our other two objectives?"

"They're covered, boss."

"How so?"

"Melvin Hinkle picked up the package about an hour ago at the Thirtieth Street Station Post Office in Philly. His instructions are to transport it to the Ardmore facility, then open it in the main laboratory. The trip switch is under the cardboard flap. I packed the box myself and shipped it by Purolator Courier. It'll happen the way we discussed—I guarantee it."

Schaulton felt reassured, but still was compelled to say, "Just like you guaranteed Hutchins?"

"Don't worry, Mr. Schaulton. I'll find him."

The idea struck him like a blow. "All right, Frankie, you get your tail over to Hancock Airport Terminal, Gate Twenty-two pronto and don't be seen. Hutchins will be there to meet me at eight-thirty. Don't give him a chance. As soon as you see him, do him. Am I making myself clear?"

"Yes," replied Frankie Pizzaro. "And the two doctors?"

"Forget them. After Hutchins, report to the usual place for full payment. Do this right, my boy, and I'll double your fee."

"Count on it, Mr. Schaulton."

"Good, Frankie. I shall."

Bertram Hollister moved slowly up to the bar at Rusty's and ordered a beer. He spotted Hutchins at a table in the rear, walked to it and sat down. "Hello there, Doctor. I'm glad you came."

Hutchins sipped his drink cautiously. The detective saw fear in his eyes.

"I've got some news for you, Hutchins. Darnell's no whacko. He *does* have your ass nailed to the wall. He and his girlfriend have isolated that protein and have determined its effects."

Silent, Hutchins raised his eyebrows.

Hollister went on, "They know that it speeds up

the aging process. They've got the dope and they're planning to finger you and Stanley Schaulton. They've pinned down the link between the two of you and Natalie Lepert. If you cooperate with me, I'll do what I can for you. Somehow, Hutchins, I just can't picture you enjoying being behind bars for the rest of your life. You scratch my back now and you've got me on your team. I think you can handle a few years in the big house—but a few decades are another story."

Hollister studied the man's face. His shock and fear were palpable. The detective knew he had touched a raw nerve. Still Hutchins said nothing.

Hollister continued, "Think about it, my friend. A couple of fucking years in Attica and your asshole'll be so wide they could drive an ATV in there, do a few wheelies and roar right out again. Is that what you want?" He paused. "Who, Dr. Hutchins, killed Natalie Lepert? Tell me and save yourself a heap of trouble."

Dr. Harold Hutchins could not believe what he was hearing. The fact that Ike Darnell and Judy Frymoyer had learned so much in such a short time astounded him. The one thing, however, that Hollister had not disclosed to him was an inkling as to the reason why the additive was used. Further, it was clear that no one had any specific idea how

Natalie was killed. To the best of his knowledge, only he and Stanley Schaulton knew those facts.

Hutchins peered into the detective's eyes and tried to guess his motivation in meeting with him. He learned nothing. Hollister was looking at him, almost tenderly, with a moist paternalism, making it seem that he was just about to break into tears.

The doctor thought of the hit man pressing the "11" button in the EconoMed elevator. *Where could he possibly have been going? If not to see me, then whom? And how the hell is Schaulton—one of the busiest guys I know—able to hop on his plane and fly to Syracuse in a moment's notice? Something stinks!*

Hutchins pondered the possibility of telling the detective everything he knew about Stanley Schaulton and EconoMed International and then simply facing the consequences *with Schaulton*. In the next moment, he reasoned that Stanley Schaulton would never go to jail, that he could be out on bail for twenty years if he wanted, but that he, Harold Hutchins, could be made to look real bad. *Would Schaulton do such a thing? Why does the EconoMed chief want to see me tonight? And the hit man—why is he in Syracuse? If Schaulton had me knocked off, would anyone be able to tie him to the additive—no matter what Darnell and his girlfriend find? Is that what's going to happen tonight at the airport?*

Hutchins had been staring into his vodka and

tonic. He looked up at Hollister and said, "Captain, there is one thing you can do for me that I would regard as a sign of good faith."

Hollister squinted and pursed his lips. "What?"

"There is a man, a dangerous man, who I believe is following me, intends to hurt me. Can you pick him up?"

"What would the charge be?"

For a split second Hutchins considered revealing what had happened in the Atlantic City hotel room, but demurred, as he had no real proof. *How about the black guy they knocked off in Wildwood? Both thugs were there—maybe this one pulled the trigger? But how do I, Dr. Harold Hutchins, know anything about that?* He realized that he could specify no charge that would stick. "Suppose he assaulted me?"

"Then I would arrest him," replied Hollister equably. "Does this guy have anything to do with Natalie Lepert's death?"

"Yes," said Hutchins, aware that he had just crossed the line. "If my suspicions are correct, he will be at Hancock Airport, Gate Twenty-two, at about eight-thirty tonight. He is short, dark curly hair, very heavily muscled, almost no visible neck, about forty-five, olive skin, could be an Italian. When I saw him this afternoon, he was wearing a tan raincoat, dark trousers and, I think, brown shoes."

"Why do you feel this guy'll be at the fucking airport tonight?" asked Bertram Hollister.

"Because that's where I'm meeting Stanley Schaulton. He's the head of EconoMed."

"And you think he'll assault you?"

"Yes. He may try to kill me."

"I'll be there, Hutchins. You can count on it."

Frankie Pizzaro passed through airport security without difficulty. He possessed no weapon capable of being picked up by a metal detector. Strolling leisurely to the end of the long ramp, he came to a T. The lower numbered gates were to the left, the others to the right. He turned right and walked to the waiting area at Gate Twenty-one, where he settled in to a red plastic seat from which he could see the doors to Gate Twenty-two.

Pizzaro looked at his watch. It was seven-fifteen. He glanced about him, noting the handful of people waiting in silence and the bored flight attendant perched behind the desk skimming a magazine. His eyes fell upon the gray-haired man sitting four rows away. He watched the man light one unfiltered cigarette with the butt of the last, reading his newspaper, looking down. Pizzaro had a bad gut feel for this guy, but didn't quite know why.

Melvin Hinkle greeted the receptionist at SAS warmly, as he crossed through the lobby carrying the large, heavy cardboard box.

"Need some help, sir?" the young woman asked.

"Nope," said Hinkle, "just ask everyone here to come into the main laboratory. I've brought their first quarter bonuses from EconoMed in Dallas."

"Bonuses? Jeeze, that box looks heavy. What's in there?"

"I'm not sure, hon. Probably something worth having. These folks are very generous."

Hinkle entered the expansive lab and placed the box down on the central counter. He heard a general page being announced to proceed at once into the lab.

After a sizable crowd had gathered, Marvin Hinkle slit the sealing tape and swung open the cardboard flaps. He heard a tiny click, then the forty pounds of plastique vaporized him and all others present. Fire blazed through the entire building within ninety seconds.

SAS Commodities, its files, its evening shift and its courier ceased to exist.

The Lear jet taxied down the runway and eased to a stop. Stanley Schaulton emerged from the passenger compartment and walked across the tarmac to Gate Twenty-two. Entering the terminal, he scanned the mostly empty seats, spied Frankie Pizzaro reading a paper in the corner, but was displeased that Hutchins was not there. From the long tunnel-way he heard the distinctive clicking of expensive shoes on the linoleum. It was Hutchins' walk; he was certain of it.

As Hutchins came into view, Schaulton caught his eye, smiled and waved. Hutchins approached, Schaulton thought, entirely too slowly, cautiously.

Schaulton saw Pizzaro lower his newspaper, stand up and move silently towards Hutchins. Then Pizzaro broke into a run and, with extraordinary grace for a man of his shape and size, leapt into the air behind Hutchins, delivering a brutal kick to the pathologist's neck. As Hutchins fell, Schaulton froze with fear.

A gray-haired man, whom he had not noticed before, jumped up, braced his pistol with both hands on the top of the plastic seat and shouted, "FREEZE, ASSHOLE! POLICE! YOU'RE UNDER ARREST!"

Frankie Pizzaro ducked and rolled towards Bertram Hollister. He came up from the floor with a hammering blow at Hollister's chest.

Hollister stepped aside, put one .357 Magnum round into his attacker's left ear, then rushed to Harold Hutchins' prone, apparently lifeless body.

In the confusion, Stanley Schaulton slipped out

the door, ran across the runway and reboarded his plane.

Ike Darnell and Judy Frymoyer were in the midst of autopsying their second dead Rhesus monkey when the lab phone rang.

Ike looked at the wall clock: almost one AM. "Judy," he said, "you'd better get it. I gave that number to Hollister."

Judy lifted the receiver, listened, then said, "It's Hollister. He wants to speak to you immediately. Says its an emergency."

Ike pulled off his bloody gloves and walked to the phone. At the end of their conversation, Ike replaced the receiver, puzzlement on his face. He said, "There's a flight to Syracuse in forty-five minutes. We're going to be on it. I'll explain later."

"I can't go, Ike. I've got to be here in the morning to examine the slides. We can't stop now. We can nail this thing right down. You go alone."

Ike Darnell kissed her, then disappeared into the night.

CHAPTER 15

11 May

Dr. Isaac Darnell eyed the immobile, unconscious patient with clinical expertise. "How bad is he, Captain?"

Bertram Hollister, standing at Ike's side, said, "I don't know the fucking medical mumbo-jumbo, but my impression is that he's got a big clot on his brain and a broken fucking neck. He's been in this coma since he got here, hasn't said a goddamned thing."

"Who's his doctor?"

"A young fellow by the name of Candless."

"I want to talk to him," said Ike.

Minutes later Darnell and Hollister walked into Dr. Evan Candless' consultation room. Candless was a tall, thin man with oversized extremities and a prominent Adam's apple. His sandy blond hair framed sharp, crisp features, deep blue eyes and a narrow-lipped mouth. The X-ray view boxes next to his desk provided the only light in the room. Candless was examining Harold Hutchins' most recent CT scan of the head and neck when the two men entered.

"Hiya, Captain," said Candless.

Hollister nodded. "Doctor, this is Dr. Ike Darnell. He's working with me on this case."

As the young neurosurgeon shook his hand, Ike saw a knowing look in his eye.

"*The* Dr. Ike Darnell?" asked Candless. "Philadelphia? Author of the best papers in the past twenty years on evacuation and laser coagulation of subdural hemotomas—the technique known to every neurosurgeon as the Darnell Procedure?"

Ike smiled bashfully, flattered that his work was so well respected outside of Philadelphia. "Good to meet you, Doctor," said Ike. "Is this Hutchins' CT?"

"It's 'Evan,' Ike, and yes, this was taken about an hour ago. We'd thought the bleeding had stopped." He placed a finger over a round white shadow on the film. "Obviously, it hasn't."

Ike studied the films. "You're right. I trust you're planning to proceed with craniotomy at once."

"Correct. In fact," said Candless, with obvious pleasure, "I was considering performing a Darnell Procedure. Care to give me a hand?"

"Would that be possible?" asked Ike excitedly, now realizing how much he'd missed clinical medicine.

"With one phone call I could get you emergency neurosurgical privileges." He placed his hand on the phone. "May I?"

Grinning, Ike nodded.

Stanley Schaulton stepped down from the veranda of his hunting camp on the Grasse River near Russell, New York and strolled into the woods. He needed desperately to think and knew that his mind would be clearer out in the fresh air and the tranquility of the wilderness.

Last night he'd ordered his pilot to make an emergency, unauthorized takeoff from Syracuse. Though he was undoubtedly tracked by radar, he was certain that, upon flying into Canadian air space, he'd foiled any pursuit or detection. The Lear jet had landed on his private air strip on a plateau in the Adirondacks near Cranberry Lake, New York, from where he'd summoned the caretaker of his camp. The old man had left him with a Jeep Wagoneer and full provisions, then had walked to his own home three miles away. Schaulton had dispatched his plane back to Dallas, not wanting to call attention to his presence. He knew that very few people were aware of the existence of this place and his connection with it. Even the caretaker did not know his real name.

Schaulton had watched the Syracuse newscast at seven AM on his cable TV and had been shocked when the broadcaster reported the killing of an unknown man by police at Hancock Airport and the *critical injuries* sustained by a local pathologist.

Knowing that Harold Hutchins was still alive forced Schaulton into a panic. He wandered down an overgrown trail ruminating about what he could possibly do to right his aborted plan. *If Hutchins talks—and he will talk if he is able—then I am finished. The stock sale will never go through and they'll come after me as an accessory to that meddling bitch's murder.*

After plodding through the woods for two hours, Schaulton returned to the log cabin, aware that he had but one option.

Pleased that he'd had the sense to have his phone service connected all year round, he picked up the receiver and placed a call to Chicago, Illinois.

Dr. Judy Frymoyer picked up the slide labeled "Brain, right frontal lobe" and placed it on the stage of her binocular microscope. She fiddled with the coarse, then the fine focus knobs. First fuzzy, then clear, the bizarre image assaulted her highly trained mind. She saw myriad birefringent fibrils scattered throughout the normal neuronal structures. *My God!* she thought. *It looks like amyloid—a highly unusual amyloid—but amyloid nonetheless!*

Feverishly, she viewed slide after slide, from kidney, liver, muscle, fat, pancreas—and each revealed the same picture.

Judy concluded that PG caused a form of multiple myeloma, a disorder of the B-lymphocytes, characterized by the unchecked synthesis of a high molecular weight protein which was deposited in every tissue in the body. The net effect was severe dysfunction of the involved organs, not unlike that seen in the tissues of extraordinarily old people.

Excited, but profoundly confused, she slumped back in her chair.

"Why?" she said aloud. "Why did they do this?"

Evan Candless raised the flap of bone and muscle, exposing the huge clot adherent to Harold Hutchins' brain. "OK, Ike," he said, handing him the laser scalpel, "it's all yours."

Deftly, Ike moved the high intensity light from the periphery of the severely injured brain tissue centrally, careful to sear each tiny bleeder he saw. After two hours of this tedious work, he scooped up the huge clot and removed it. He examined the crushed, bruised and swollen tissue beneath it and said, "Most of his occipital lobe has been destroyed. If he survives, he'll probably be blind."

Candless nodded.

Ike said, "The field looks dry. Let's close, then explore his spinal fracture. If the CT's accurate, his cord's been severed. He'll be a quadriplegic."

From the observation gallery high above the operating theater, Ike heard Hollister ask, "If he wakes up, Ike, will he be able to talk?"

"Yes," replied Ike, "it's likely that he will, *if* he wakes up."

Immediately after the noon news Stanley Schaulton called Hiram Folger in Dallas. He was put right through to the lawyer. "Hiram, it's Stan. How are you coming with the stock sale?"

"Terrific!" Folger said exuberantly. "I contacted Tony Marin, the investment banker with Morgan Guaranty, and he believes he's got a buyer for every last share."

"Who?" asked Schaulton incredulously, surprised that someone that wealthy had been located so quickly.

"A Saudi syndicate. They've been interested in a takeover like this for months. Apparently one of their sheiks has a son he wants working every day. They wish to install him as CEO of EconoMed."

Schaulton thought, *This is beautiful. Now if I can just take care of Hutchins, I'll be all set.* He said,

"Hiram, how long will it take you to consummate this deal?"

"Marin's meeting with a representative of the syndicate tomorrow morning. If they can agree on a buy-out price per share, then we can close promptly."

"How promptly?"

"Stan, the stock's trading at forty-nine and has a book value of sixty. Marin thinks he can get the syndicate to go for ninety-five bucks a share. If that's suitable, two, maybe three days."

Schaulton smiled. He owned 78.3 million shares. The prospect of having seven and a half billion dollars deposited into his Swiss account quickened his pulse. "Tell Marin to proceed expeditiously, Hiram. I don't want any time wasted. Clear?"

"Perfectly," said the lawyer.

Schaulton told him that he'd changed his plans slightly, gave him his present phone number and rang off.

He called Jessica Pahler's apartment in Chicago and was pleased to get no answer.

With nine of the remaining monkeys seriously ill with a variety of unlikely disorders, Judy Frymoyer was swamped caring for them. She had just drawn multiple blood specimens for analysis from the sickest of them, when she realized that she hadn't eaten breakfast or lunch.

Passing through the line of the staff dining hall, she carried her tray towards an empty table. "Judy," she heard from behind her, "why don't you join me?"

She spun around and saw Dean Jeffrey Palmer eating alone. Palmer was a short, stout man in his mid-fifties with thin, graying hair which topped an aristocratic face. She came to his table, placed down her tray and sat down.

"My God, Doctor! You look exhausted. What's got you so wound up?" asked Palmer.

Between bites of her BLT and potato chips, Judy gave Palmer a summary of her PG experiments. Sipping his coffee, the Dean listened intently without speaking.

When she'd finished, Palmer said, "What you're saying is extraordinary. If we were to use such a protein for research purposes, we just might be able to unravel the mysteries of aging."

Judy nodded, munching her chocolate eclair. The same thought had occurred to her.

"Who owns the process?" asked Palmer.

Judy realized that, in order to answer this question truthfully, she'd have to reveal the results of Ike's investigation and the relationship of PG to the murders of Natalie Lepert and Peter Tillers. Jeff Palmer was her friend. She decided to tell him.

"You must never repeat what I'm about to tell you," she said. "Agreed?"

Palmer looked at her strangely, then: "You've got my word."

"Have you ever heard of EconoMed International?"

"Of course. It's the largest health care provider in the world. I own stock in the company."

Judy told him what she knew about Natalie Lepert, Peter Tillers and Harold Hutchins, including what she'd learned from Ike by phone this morning—that Hutchins was hospitalized with severe neurological damage. She continued, "Both Ike and Captain Hollister believe that the mastermind behind the whole operation is EconoMed's head man, a guy by the name of Stanley Schaulton."

Palmer winced as though slapped. "*Stanley Schaulton?* Don't you think they're jumping to erroneous conclusions? Schaulton's one of the richest men in the world. Why would he—why would anybody—add a protein to allergenic extracts which promoted premature aging? It doesn't add up."

"That, Jeff, we don't know."

"You'd better think this through more carefully, Judy, before making any accusations. Remember, you've now involved the reputation of Yale University. Further, you should know that Schaulton is not only one of our biggest contributors, but he's also a personal friend of mine. Whatever you do, don't piss him off."

Seeing the fire in Palmer's eyes, Judy was silent. As the Dean arose to leave, she asked, "How do you know Mr. Schaulton?"

"We deer hunt together every fall. He owns property adjacent to mine in St. Lawrence County in upstate New York. Good afternoon, Doctor," Palmer said coolly, "and don't forget what I said."

Ike Darnell stood with Evan Candless at Harold Hutchins' bedside in the surgical ICU of University Hospital. Ike noted the even cadence of Hutchins' cardiac monitor and his regular respirations. He heard Candless ask him, "How long do you think we should continue the IV steroids?"

"A minimum of seventy-two hours. The acute swelling of his brain should have abated by then, though he might regain consciousness at any time."

"Thanks for your help, Ike. We might have lost him in the OR without it."

"It's a pleasure, Evan." He moved towards the door. "Do me a favor?"

"Name it."

"If Hutchins wakes up, call me immediately. I'll be at the police station with Captain Hollister."

"You'll be the first to know."

Ike walked quickly out of the hospital and caught a cab downtown. Entering Hollister's office, he found the detective tapping at the keys of a personal computer, one that had clearly been set up on his desk recently.

"Know anything about these goddamned things, Ike?"

"A little. What are you up to?"

Hollister explained that, at Sophie Lepert's suggestion, he'd searched through her husband's documents and had found four diskettes labeled "Natalie/Backup 01" through "Natalie/Backup 04" in the box marked "2nd Quarter" of the year she was killed.

Surprised, Ike said, "I looked through all those boxes, Captain—especially that one—and I didn't find a thing."

"The box had a false bottom—a piece of cardboard set in under all the documents. The diskettes were glued to the underside of the cardboard. Remember, Ike, I'm a cop."

Ike was excited. "What's on them?"

"I don't fucking know. Each diskette has one file on it called 'Backup.' My man downstairs helped me do something called 'Restoring' them to the hard disk, but they're all coded."

"Coded?"

"Yeh. Just numbers and fucking dots."

"I'm no expert, but I'd say we'd be much more

likely to be able to read them if we used the same software program as Natalie Lepert did."

Hollister considered this, then nodded.

Ike smiled. "May I use your phone?"

Hollister offered the receiver.

Ike found the number, dialed it and waited to be connected. While on hold, he said, "Hutchins is still comatose. He might wake up in ten minutes; he might never. We're just going to—"

He heard the familiar voice say, "Shearson Lehman Hutton. This is Tracey Barr. May I help you?"

"Tracey, this is Ike Darnell."

"Hello, Doctor. What can I do for you?"

"You told me before that you had seen Natalie backing up her hard disk onto diskettes—correct?"

"Correct. Many times."

"Do you happen to remember what software program she used?"

"Sure. She had a word processing program called 'Multi-Mate.'"

"You're terrific, Tracey. Thanks very much."

"Is that all, Doctor. I thought you might be calling me about the takeover rumors on Econo-Med International. It's a great buy. You could make a bundle. Sure I can't interest you?"

Ike's face narrowed. "I thought Stanley Schaulton owned most of the stock?"

"He does, but rumor on Wall Street has it that Schaulton's become ill and is selling out."

Ike said, "Could you hold the wire for a moment, Tracey?"

"Sure."

Ike turned to Hollister. "Captain, you said that Hutchins was planning to meet Schaulton when he was attacked."

"Yes, that's what he told me."

"Did you see Schaulton there?"

"Ike, I wouldn't know Stanley Schaulton if I fell over him. There was, however, an older man standing in the doorway when that shithead kicked Hutchins. It could've been Schaulton, but after I'd shot the guy, I looked up and the old guy was gone."

Ike uncovered the mouthpiece of the phone. "Tracey, is it possible for you to put your hands on a photograph of Schaulton?"

"I don't see why not. Shearson's got a huge business library at the World Trade Center. They've got dossiers on every major CEO in the world. When do you need it?"

"Now."

"OK, I'll request a fax and run it down to you as soon as I get it. Where are you?"

"Captain Hollister's office at the police station. Tracey, you're terrific." Ike hung up.

"What was that all about?" asked Hollister.

Ike explained.

"All right," said the detective. "Let's get a copy of this Multi-Mate and find out what the fuck's on these diskettes."

"Good idea," said Ike. "But there's one other thing. Assuming that the guy you saw *was* Schaulton, do you think you can find out if he filed a flight plan to Syracuse and whether he gave a destination when he left?"

"I'll call my friends at the airport," said Bertram Hollister.

Dr. Jessica Pahler sat peacefully in the main lobby of University Hospital. She was a pretty brunette. Tall and exquisitely built, with high cheekbones, perfect teeth and smooth skin, she looked now at forty-five a full ten years younger. Throughout her adult life, especially during her many psychiatric hospitalizations, she had overheard comments by numerous men about how it was so tragic for such a beautiful woman to be so crazy. After completing her Ph.D. in Pharmacology at Harvard, she had experimented with several of the hallucinogens she was studying. She'd never been the same. Stanley Schaulton had made her acquaintance ten years ago while visiting a young lady friend of his at the McLean Psychiatric Hospital in central Massachusetts. He'd discovered her hidden talents and purchased them from time to time.

Jessica scanned the flow of traffic through the

lobby, noting that, as at most teaching hospitals, individuals wearing white coats with stethoscopes stuffed in their pockets could go anywhere without question.

She left the hospital and, finding a uniform and supply shop one block away, purchased the necessary paraphernalia.

Jessica returned to University Hospital, entered the ground floor ladies' room, changed her clothes, then moved with the flow of the crowd into the elevator.

She walked swiftly into the Surgical ICU, knowing that sheer boldness was critical. Stopping at the chart rack, she located Harold Hutchins' chart and flipped through it.

No one said a word to her.

Jessica stopped briefly outside the door to Room Eight, surveyed it thoroughly, then exited the ICU.

Dr. Jessica Pahler made her way to her hotel room to make final preparations. She had already decided precisely how to kill Harold Hutchins.

Ike Darnell opened the brown envelope and thrust onto Hollister's desk the eight by ten glossy of a well-preserved, distinguished-looking man dressed in a dark three piece business suit. "Is that the guy?" he asked.

"Sure is."

Ike had just returned from the nearest ComputerLand where he'd purchased Multi-Mate, when Tracey Barr met him in the lobby and gave him the envelope. He set the box containing the program down on the desk. "Any word from the airport, Captain?"

"Yes. Schaulton owns a Lear jet. He was scheduled to land in Syracuse at eight-thirty last night. The air traffic controllers confirmed that he *did* land at eight-twenty-five. Four minutes later an unidentified jet, believed to be Schaulton's, took off without authorization, nearly colliding with a Delta 727 headed for Boston. The craft was tracked by radar over Lake Ontario and into Canada, but they fucking lost it about ten minutes after passing over Kingston."

"So we've lost him?" asked Ike.

"Yes and no. Forty-five minutes ago the FAA confirmed that Schaulton's plane was sitting in his private hangar near Dallas, adjacent to his residence. They obtained a federal search warrant, but the airstrip and his home were empty. The plane's been impounded, but Schaulton's whereabouts are unknown."

Ike was pensive. "Why do you think he ran?"

"I can only fucking conjecture."

"Conjecture."

"Based upon what Hutchins told me in the bar, I think Schaulton lured him into a trap at the airport so his goon could off him. He never expected me to be there to protect Hutchins. Schaulton saw what went down, panicked, then went into hiding. My guess is—especially after hearing what Tracey Barr said—that he plans to liquidate his assets, sever his relationship with Econo-Med, then get the fuck out of American jurisdiction. Remember, there's a warrant out for his arrest."

"Makes sense," said Ike, "but he'd have to use a commercial airline to get to Europe, Mexico or Asia. And with the feds after him, he'd be nailed. I think he's still in the States or in Canada, just biding his time until his stock's sold. Let's see if he's got a hideaway somewhere. A man of his wealth must have such a place."

"You're probably right, but we're talking about one fuck of a lot of acres. We'll never find him. Look, let's see what's on these diskettes. There may be a clue."

Ike was just booting the program when Evan Candless called and told him that Harold Hutchins had come out of his coma and was talking.

Darnell and Hollister entered the darkened room with Evan Candless. Ike's eyes adjusted to the dim light and he saw a strange woman sitting at the bedside holding the patient's hand. "Who's that?" he whispered to Candless.

"His wife. She's been here all day. Hutchins has been babbling on and off for the past ten minutes. They've been talking about their kids."

Hollister thrust his head close to the other two men. "Any chance we could speak with him alone, Doctor?"

"Let me see what I can do," said Candless, moving toward the grief-stricken woman. After a few simple words, he ushered her out of the room.

Ike stood on one side of the bed; Hollister on the other. "Doctor Hutchins," said the detective, "it's Captain Hollister. Can you hear me?"

Hutchins' dry tongue protruded from his mouth and struck the nasogastric tube taped to his nose. His eyes were wide and glazed. A spherical metal restraint immobilized his head and neck, lateral skewers seemingly embedded into his scalp on either side. "Yes," he said faintly.

"I want you to tell me about Natalie Lepert."

"Whaddyawanna know?"

Ike saw that Hollister's eyes narrowed, that his face contracted. He watched him lean close to the pathologist's face. "Who killed her?" asked Hollister.

"I did."

"How?"

"Tampons."

Suddenly, it occurred to Ike that the vaginal mucosa allowed transport of medications directly into the bloodstream, much in the same way as rectal suppositories or sublingual nitroglycerine tablets. He bent down. "What was in the tampons?" asked Ike.

"Potassium chloride. Two hundred milliequivalents each. I slipped them into her purse."

"Why?" asked Hollister. "Why did you kill her?"

Hutchins' tongue probed the air again, rolled jerkily on cracked lips, retracted into his mouth. He coughed. His voice became raspy and more difficult to understand. "One weekend I took her to the camp in the woods. Schaulton let us use it. He keeps the formulae for synthesis of the additive there, locked in a safe hidden underneath the fireplace. I'd had too much wine. Natalie and I'd been screwing. She found a sheet of paper Schaulton must've left out. Asked me. I was drunk. Told her what the additive did, but not what we used it for. Next morning I knew I'd made a mistake. She asked a lot of questions, kept rambling about her Dad. I pretended I didn't know what she was talking about."

Excited, Ike inquired, "When was that?"

"Late winter," replied the tiring Hutchins. "Maybe early spring. Snow was just melting." He coughed again, this time more deeply. His entire flaccid body rippled on the egg-crate mattress. Quieting, he said, "She didn't mention it again 'till the summer, asked me directly if her Dad was getting

217

the additive in his allergy shots at EconoMed. I told Schaulton. He had some nut case from Chicago mail me the tampons. Said Natalie had to be terminated—maybe me too, if I didn't cooperate."

Ike saw a tall brunette nurse enter the room. He heard her say, "Excuse me, gentlemen, but this man needs his meds."

"Go ahead and give them," said Ike, annoyed at this interruption at so critical a time.

Bertram Hollister asked, "Hutchins, where is this camp?"

The nurse inserted a needle into a port on Harold Hutchins' IV line and depressed the plunger rapidly.

"Upstate New York. Foothills of the Adirondacks. Near a little town called—"

Harold Hutchins' lips stopped moving. His cardiac monitor began to race wildly, setting off strident alarms. The heave of his chest ceased.

Ike immediately initiated mouth-to-mouth resuscitation and closed chest massage.

The nurse moved slowly to the doorway. Hollister spun to face her.

She raised a straw-like object to her lips and blew forcefully. A tiny dart zipped across the tiny room with a *pffffftttt* and impaled Hollister in the left chest.

The detective reached into his jacket and withdrew his pistol. "FREEZE, LADY!" he screamed, rasing the gun into firing position.

The brunette brought another white tube to her lips. She was five feet from the police captain.

"DROP IT!" shrieked Hollister.

She inhaled deeply.

Bertram Hollister shot her in the mouth, blowing off the back of her head. Brain tissue splattered onto the glass partition. The brunette slumped to the floor.

As the arrest team stormed into the room, Hollister plucked the small dart from his jacket, realizing that its penetration had been stymied by his gold detective's shield.

Five minutes later, amidst the ineffable chaos in Room Eight of the Surgical ICU, Ike Darnell stepped back from the bed and said, "Captain, Hutchins is dead."

The two men left University Hospital and drove to the police station.

Exhausted, Judy Frymoyer switched off her microscope light, hung her white coat on the hook and walked to her apartment. She thought that a shower and a meal might energize her and enable her to return to the lab for the rest of the evening.

The hot needles of water pelting her skin, her mind drifted to Ike Darnell. Judy stepped out of the shower, toweled off and phoned Hollister's office in

Syracuse. Thirty seconds later she heard Ike's calm, friendly voice, "Judy, you're not going to believe what's happened up here."

"Try me," she said, cleaning her ears with Q-tips. She listened attentively to Ike's narration, then heard him conclude with: "So how's it going in the lab?"

"Seven more monkeys have died—two from heart disease, one from a stroke, one from liver failure and one from uremia. I haven't determined the last." Judy kept the cordless phone under her chin and wandered into the living room. Absently, she turned on the television set, volume on low, and saw the local news anchor's face appear. "Ike, the microscopic findings are just what I'd expected and then some. There's an unusual protein, something like amyloid, deposited in every organ of every animal."

"Amyloid?" queried Ike. "That's a damn rare bird."

"True, but—" Judy stopped in mid-sentence, seeing a picture flash on the TV screen of a distinguished gentleman with "STANLEY SCHAULTON" superimposed under it in white, block letters. "Just a minute, Ike!" Judy put down the phone and grabbed the remote control box from the coffee table, turning up the volume.

She heard: " —and it's believed that the multi-billionaire tycoon directed his Lear jet to make an unauthorized takeoff from the Syracuse airport, nearly resulting in a midair collision with a commercial aircraft. The federal government has issued a warrant for Schaulton's arrest for questioning into the matter, but Schaulton remains at large at this hour. Turning to local—" Judy silenced the set and picked up the cordless. "Ike, are you aware that Stanley Schaulton is a wanted man?"

"Sorry, I guess I forgot to mention that. The FAA's after him."

Judy said excitedly, "You told me that Hutchins took Natalie Lepert to a camp somewhere. Could it be Schaulton's place?"

"Probably was."

"Do you think that's where Schaulton is now?"

"Good chance, but Hutchins never got the opportunity to finish. There must be thousands of places like that in the Adirondacks. We'd never find him."

"I think I know how we might locate it. The Dean of the Yale Med School, Jeff Palmer, told me today at lunch that he hunts with Schaulton every fall and owns a place adjacent to his."

"Where, Judy?"

Judy strained to recall Palmer's last words to her. She smiled. "His place is somewhere in St. Lawrence County. Does that mean anything to you?"

"Ogdensburg's in St. Lawrence County. What's your Dean's full name?"

"Palmer. Dr. Jeffrey Palmer."

Ike wrote the name on the pad he'd been scribbling on. "Why don't you ask Palmer exactly where his place is?"

Judy recalled Palmer's frosty tone at the end of their conversation. "I don't believe he'd help us, Ike. Apparently, Schaulton's a big contributor to Yale and a good friend of his. Jeff sounded awfully protective of him."

"Not even with a federal warrant out for Schaulton's arrest?"

"No," said Judy. "I don't think so."

"All right, Judy. Let me think this through. The Captain found Natalie's diskettes at her mother's home. We're just about to scan them. Look, why don't you climb into bed and get some rest. You've gotten more than enough information from those monkeys to hang EconoMed and Schaulton. And now with Hutchins' statement, Hollister's trying to get a local judge to issue another warrant for Schaulton as an accessory in the murder of Natalie Lepert. Sleep well. I'll call you in the morning."

The woods surrounding Stanley Schaulton's camp were noisy with wildlife. A doe who had just dropped her fawn stood outside the huge bay window, nursing her baby and staring into the brightly lit room.

Schaulton gulped the last of his scotch and said into his telephone, "Damnit, Hiram, why won't they come across?"

"Stan, haven't you read the papers or seen the news?"

"No, I've been out in the woods all day thinking. What's happened?"

"Your picture's in every paper. The feds are claiming that your plane violated commercial air space. The Saudis stopped payment on their check. I called Tony Marin in New York and he said they think you're scamming them."

"That's complete bullshit, Hiram, and you know it. You saw Dr. Woodley's report. My ticker's on the fritz and I'm just getting out. Why don't you call Marin and see if he can rustle up some Japs? They've been anxious as hell for years to get a piece of EconoMed."

"Stan, I'm afraid you're screwed until you can clear this FAA thing. No one's going to touch your holdings with a ten-foot pole. According to Marin, the stock's going to fall through the floor at the opening bell tomorrow." Hiram Folger paused and awaited Schaulton's remarks. He heard nothing. "Stan, look, if there's anything I can do to help you, you let me know. 'Kay?"

Thirty seconds passed.

"Stan?"

"I'm here."

"Is there anything you want me to do?"

"Yes. Don't tell anyone where I am or how to reach me." Schaulton hung up the phone.

He poured himself another scotch from the decanter at the elaborate, well-stocked bar. He drank heavily into the night, thinking about his humble start in life, his meteoric rise to the top, his chance meeting of a lovely biochemist in a Houston singles' bar, his decision to take the woman's discovery and her life from her, then to implement his profitable scheme at the expense of thousands of lives. *And now I suppose I deserve what I'm going to get—public disgrace, maybe time in jail, possibly a return to being a pauper . . . unless, of course, I should have the chance to silence that meddling Darnell, his girlfriend and his police buddy—but I'll probably never see them again.*

Profoundly depressed, Schaulton turned on his TV set and watched the news. He verified that what Hiram Folger had told him was true.

He also learned that Harold Hutchins was dead.

Stanley Schaulton fell asleep in his chair, stuporously drunk.

Bertram Hollister peered through red eyes at the blue screen with the green letters on it. Ike sat next to him, equally fatigued. They had scanned the first three diskettes and had found little of significance—mostly personal correspondence, journal articles and financial records.

Ike popped in the fourth and restored it to memory. He directed the computer to "Edit a Document" mode and stared at the names of the various files: *"DAD-1"* through *"DAD-32"* . . . *"HAMBLY-1," "HAMBLY-2"* . . . *"STILES DUST"* . . . *"TILLERS"* . . . *"PRO-GERIATRIN-1"* through *"PRO-GERIATRIN-18."*

"Holy fucking shit," whispered Bertram Hollister. "We should've been smart enough to look at this one first."

They pored through the dead pathologist's notes until their eyes closed and they slept.

CHAPTER 16

12 May

Stanley Schaulton awakened at ten-thirty AM stiff, sore and hung over. He walked out into the clearing, urinated on the lawn, then found the local phone directory. Through bleary eyes he dialed the Shearson office in Potsdam, New York and asked to speak with any available broker.

"Chip Daniels, may I help you?"

"Yes, this is Herman Heintz," said Schaulton, using the name he'd been given at birth. "I'm visiting the area and wonder if you could give me some info on a stock."

"That's my business, Mr. Heintz. Which stock?"

"EconoMed International."

Daniels burst out laughing. He regained control and said, "Sorry, but all hell's broken loose with EconoMed."

"It was at an even fifty yesterday," said Schaulton. "Where's it now?"

"As of five minutes ago it was thirty-one and still dropping—thanks to good old Stanley Schaulton, who, not incidentally, has just lost a billion and a half dollars on paper in two hours. Listen, Mr. Heintz, this Schaulton fellow's probably on the up and up and this whole mess may straighten out in a few days. A shrewd investor would look upon this as a good opportunity to buy. Interested?"

"GO SCREW YOURSELF!" screeched Schaulton, slamming down the phone.

For the first time in more than fifty years Stanley Schaulton felt helpless. He unlocked his gun cabinet and removed two .44 Magnum pistols and a seven millimeter ought eight high-powered rifle. Schaulton carefully selected the proper ammunition, a double holster and a rifle sling and fitted his gear to his body.

The decision to commit suicide he'd already made. Schaulton's main concern now was how and where. He thought of the place where he usually sat during hunting season, a rocky hillock over on Jeff Palmer's property which afforded a magnificent view of three huge gullies and, in the distance, much of the St. Lawrence River valley. He loved that spot, especially the small clearing amid the copse of pines at the very top.

It'd be a good place to die, he thought, heading into the forest at a brisk pace.

Bertram Hollister parked the four wheel drive Bronco he'd borrowed from his desk sergeant in front of the county Court House in Canton, New York. He got out and walked with Ike Darnell into the main foyer. Seeing the receptionist, he approached, asked where the township maps were kept and was directed into a huge, dusty room filled with thousands of oversized, tattered books.

It took Hollister and Darnell forty minutes to find the surveyor's map which contained Dr. Jeffrey Palmer's property.

Ike took out his pad and pen and made a rough sketch of the relevant area. "Must be," he whispered to the detective, "either this one marked 'D. Lovely' or this massive tract marked 'H. Heintz.' What do you think, Captain?"

Bertram Hollister was exhausted. Though in his late sixties, he'd always pushed himself like a much younger man. Today, however, he wished he'd never started smoking and had continued to play handball twice a week as he used to. After three and a half hours' sleep, Hollister had acquiesced to Ike's suggestion to search for Stanley Schaulton. Ike had argued that, though they now knew who killed Natalie Lepert, they did not really know why. Her records had revealed many details of the substance given to her father in his allergy shots—what she had called "Progeriatrin"—but not why EconoMed, presumably at Schaulton's direction, had chosen to administer it. She had alluded to an economic motive, but she'd left it vague and undeveloped. Darnell's curiosity had infected him. Further, Hollister wanted desperately to collar Schaulton for the murder.

They descended into the basement of the Court House and walked into the sheriff's office. Armed with complicated directions taking them over logging roads and mere trails, they set out for Russell.

Ike was tensely excited. He studied the passing foliage with great anticipation. Neither man spoke until they saw the wooden sign which said: **j. PALMER PRIVATE NO TRESPASSING.**

"Look up there, Ike," said Hollister pointing. "From that knoll we'd have a great view of the Lovely property to the east and Heintz's in the other direction."

Ike nodded.

Hollister parked the Bronco next to Palmer's ultra-modern redwood-covered dwelling. Chatting amiably, they marched on foot the half mile up to the knoll.

Oblivious to the chirping birds and the small animals in the brush, Schaulton sprawled on the soft bed of pine needles and stared vacantly into the pellucidly azure sky, ruminating about his stellar rise and precipitous fall. He knew that he had all the time in the world. When the moment to place the barrel of the pistol to his temple and squeeze the trigger came, he would do it without hesitation.

But his macabre thoughts seemed to postpone that act. He had found a special peace and would luxuriate in it during the last hours of his life. He relived in his mind his entire life, smiling, crying, laughing, deeply touched by that perspective. That instant of the end—it could wait.

Deep in introspection, in a kind of fugue, he heard the voices approaching in the distance.

Though his head still throbbed, Schaulton arose swiftly and ducked back behind a huge boulder at the edge of the clearing. He rested the rifle on a shelf of rock and peered through the scope— the entire area at the top of the hillock was in view.

Schaulton waited.

The voices became louder.

Closer.

He heard the men's footsteps and felt their vibrations beneath his own feet.

A gray-haired man stepped to the brink of the precipice and scanned the area below to the west— Schaulton's own land. Schaulton recognized him immediately as the policeman who had shot Frankie Pizzaro at Hancock Airport. Heart pounding, Schaulton placed the cross-hairs over the man's right ear. His index finger flexed over the trigger.

See you in hell, partner! thought Stanley Schaulton, but in the instant before he would pull the trigger, he saw a rear view of a second man.

Halting, he lingered until the man's face was clear. The man turned towards the massive boulder.

Stanley Schaulton was ecstatic. *Wo, ho, ho,* he thought, *he's black and he's big—got to be Ike Darnell!*

Schaulton re-aimed the rifle, inhaled deeply and pulled the trigger.

Ike Darnell felt the rippling motion of the air in front of his face before he heard the gun shot. He saw Hollister fall to the ground and followed suit. "Captain? Are you OK?" yelled Ike, his voice echoing bizarrely around him.

On his knees, deep in the pine needles, Ike moved closer to the detective and realized that he'd pulled his gun and was looking warily in the direction of the boom. "You hit, Ike?" asked Hollister.

"No. You?"

"No, but some fucking asshole is *real* close to us."

"Drop your gun and don't make any fast moves," said Stanley Schaulton calmly from his vantage twelve feet away.

Hollister looked in the direction of the voice, holding on to his pistol.

Schaulton fired again, placing the bullet a half inch from Ike Darnell's left knee.

"NOW!" shrieked Schaulton.

Hollister flipped the .357 Magnum into the pine needles.

"How about you, *Doctor?*" asked Schaulton.

"I'm not armed," said Ike.

"Who are you and what do you want?" asked Hollister in a low, soft, non-provocative tone.

Schaulton ripped off another round, this one slicing into the padded shoulder of the detective's tan sports jacket and grazing his skin. An enlarging red circle appeared.

Jolted by a surge of adrenalin, Schaulton's mind spun. A plan of sorts congealed there. He said, "On your feet! Walk to the edge of the clearing and stop at that red maple. NOW!"

Ike helped Hollister up and made a cursory examination of his wound, then led him to the maple tree, next to which began a trail down a small hill.

Schaulton pranced from his hiding place and strode into the open. Holding the two men at gun point, he directed them to walk down the trail without turning around.

Thirty minutes later they came to another clearing. Ike spied a Jeep Wagoneer with New York plates parked next to a luxurious, all stone summer home. He had not seen the man who'd forced them here, but he had felt his footsteps and heard his breathing every inch of the way. Ike had stopped being terrified and was now trying to create scenarios in his mind which would eventuate in his and Hollister's escape. He was sure the detective was doing the same.

Ike had perceived the Texas drawl in the man's voice. Further, he was not pleased that the man seemed to know him. *Has to be Stanley Schaulton!* he reasoned. He knew, therefore, that the man was desperate, that time was not his or Hollister's ally.

"Up those steps onto the porch," Ike heard from behind.

They complied and came to three outdoor metal chairs, rusted and partly wet. "OK, Copper, you sit in the blue one. Darnell, there's a hank of twine on that ledge. Tie him good. Wrists and ankles. I want some real fancy surgical knots."

After Ike had knotted Hollister's extremities to the chair, he heard the man he knew to be Schaulton say, "Good. Now pull the red chair six feet from your friend and sit in it."

Schaulton came to a spot on the porch midway between the two men. He lifted the spool of twine and fashioned a loop, then commanded that Ike extend his arms.

Damn! I've got no choice. He's got a pistol six inches from the Captain's head. Ike allowed his arms, then his legs to be bound and tied.

Stanley Schaulton sat on the porch railing facing his prisoners. He held a .44 Magnum pistol in each hand, trained on the chests of Darnell and Hollister. "Let me introduce myself, gentlemen. My name is Stanley Schaulton. Now you, *sir*, I know, are Dr. Isaac Darnell. But you, piddleface," he said turning towards the detective, "I want you to identify yourself. I saw you gun down Frankie Pizzaro, so I know you're a cop." Schaulton paused, then pulled back the hammer of the pistol nearest the bleeding man.

"I am Detective Captain Bertram Hollister, Syracuse Police Department."

"Aha!" shrieked Schaulton. "A big shot police detective. Think you're pretty darned smart, don't you? How come you never figured out who killed the girl?"

"You mean Natalie Lepert?" asked Hollister.

"That's right."

"We know how she died, Schaulton, but not why," said Hollister evenly. "Care to fill us in?"

"Why, why, why, why, why?" cooed Schaulton.

"Oh, that's a wonderful word—so full and rich of meaning. Why? You want to know why?"

"Yes," said Ike. "You're going to kill us anyway, so what does it matter?"

Schaulton laughed, so hard that his hands shook and tears leaked from his eyes. "You're a real smart aleck, Darnell—and you're right. I *am* going to blow the crap out of you two for what you've done to me." Schaulton waved the guns in the air before him, then stopped, sucked in air and said, "I want you two to know that you're listening to a damned business genius, a guy who turned nothing into everything. Well, it all had to do with this protein."

"We know about the protein, Schaulton," said Hollister. "Further, we know that it causes rapid, progressive aging. What we don't understand is why it was given to EconoMed patients in their allergy shots."

As Hollister spoke, Ike exerted whatever force he could muster without being seen on the thick twine that bound him. He thought he felt a loosening of his left wrist.

Schaulton pursed his lips and blinked several times before responding. "All right, fellows. Now listen real good. This is pure genius. First off, Darnell, what can you tell me about HMO's?"

"They're prepaid health plans. A family pays a fixed number of dollars per year. They get charged the same whether they use the plan's services a hundred times or never. The plan has to take care of all their health care needs."

Schaulton fell back into his businessman voice, one devoid of the precipitous highs and lows he'd just been using. "That's true of most HMO's, Darnell, but not EconoMed. We were smart and I had the additive."

"How was yours different?" asked Hollister.

"In every policy there was a clause in fine print, which specified that, in the event that a policy holder's liability totalled more than thirty thousand dollars in a given calendar year, that person would be responsible for twenty-five per cent of all fees above that level."

"A hidden co-pay for catastrophic claims?" asked Ike.

"You got it. Once a patient was hospitalized, our staff could run his tab over thirty G's in a week or less. From that point on, we really padded the bills—expensive blood tests, MRI's, x-rays, consultations, the works. If somebody had a chronic, debilitating illness, he and his family were usually looking at *months*, very *expensive* months, in the hospital."

Hollister's eyes glared. "So you were charging yourselves the seventy-five per cent—a wash—and scamming those poor fuckers for the rest."

"Precisely."

"So you had them signing up in droves," said Ike, now beginning to appreciate the venal cleverness of the scam, "appealing to the fact that most people would consider dirt-cheap routine health care a big plus, never really believing they'd be sick enough to get into the co-pay bracket."

"Assuming, of course," interjected Hollister, "they'd bothered to read the fucking fine print."

"Of course," said Schaulton, a wicked crazy smile on his face, an eldritch glow in his eyes.

Hollister shook his head dejectedly. More blood spurted from his injured shoulder. "You fucking greedy son of a bitch!"

Schaulton nodded exuberantly. "And that's where the additive came in. Almost a third of the health care bill in the United States is spent taking care of patients *during their last ninety days of life*! That's where the big money is. We initiated the pilot program in the allergy shots just to see if those patients developed age-related diseases more quickly. It paid off in spades. Two years after we'd begun, our profits were up three hundred per cent. Every damn one of our hospital facilities was *full all the time*. We launched into phase two with a massive building program, constructing six hundred new inpatient facilities across the country. That was a year ago. Three months ago we began to put the additive into eye drops, sublingual nitro tabs, insulin, B 12 shots, cortisone vials, rectal and vaginal suppositories—any vehicle that could deliver the protein into the bloodstream. Of course, we continued using it in the allergy shots. Our stock, gentlemen, our stock took off like a darned—" Schaulton began to weep, blubber like a baby.

Ike kept up the tension on his right wrist bond. It loosened enough for him to reach across the bottom of the chair. He began to untie his left.

"And then you, YOU INTERFERING SON OF A BITCH, started digging into the death of the Lepert girl. And now I ask you, before I blow your crap-filled brains out, WHY? Why did you give a whit about her?"

As Ike worked on the twine, his mind drifted back to the Bellevue-Stratford Ballroom. To the six shots. To the brains of his daughter slopping on the shrimp cocktail. To the emptiness in his life. To the pleading eyes of an old woman who wondered why her daughter had died—wanting him to find out. He thought of Judy. Her warm body, her tender caresses.

The porch fell into the afternoon shadows; the darkness assisted Ike's efforts with the twine.

"WHY? YOU GODDARNED UPPITY ARSE-HOLE! WHY?" shrilled Stanley Schaulton, who then spun toward Hollister. "AND YOU—WHY DID YOU DESTROY MY LIFE?"

Hollister, now weakening, said, "I'm a cop,

Schaulton. You. You're fucking scum. My job is to clean up the scum on this earth."

Schaulton raised both pistols, pointed them in the air, then at Darnell and Hollister, then at himself, then back at them. His sobbing worsened. "I'm a genius. A genius. A BLOODY GENIUS! I turned a two-bit bankrupt HMO into a MULTI-BILLION DOLLAR BUSINESS!" His weeping overcame him. Schaulton placed one of the pistols on the railing and wiped his nose with his sleeve.

Ike pulled with all his might. The twine snapped. His hands were free. Using a gentle rocking motion he moved his chair ten inches closer to Schaulton. He was within reach.

Dry-eyed, Schaulton picked up the second pistol. He turned to Hollister. "I'm going to put you out of your misery first. Scum? You dare to call Stanley Schaulton scum?" He raised the .44 in his right hand and pulled back the hammer. Schaulton pointed it at Bertram Hollister's nose. "I'm not sorry to see you go, you sassy—"

Ike snapped up. He brought both of his huge arms down upon Schaulton's. The gun in his right discharged, blowing a hole in the deck. The other Magnum struck the wooden floor and bounded over the edge.

Ike tried to stand to gain leverage, but his bound legs prevented that. He stumbled and rolled into Schaulton's shins, the metal chair laced to his calves.

Schaulton grasped the rail for balance. He did not fall.

Ike looked up and was horrified.

His heart triphammered in his chest.

Stanley Schaulton still held the one .44 Magnum pistol. He pointed it at Ike. "My Daddy told me never to trust a black. PAPA, YOU WERE RIGHT!" he screamed.

Ike heard the click of the hammer.

"OH, PAPA, YOU WERE RIGHT!"

In that instant Ike saw his wife and daughters die a thousand times, heard those six shots from Vinny Parisi's gun a million times, made love to Judy Frymoyer a billion times.

He waited for the explosion he would never hear.

Then, in the distance, heralded and shielded by the bright afternoon sun, Ike heard, "DROP IT, STAN! DON'T BE A FOOL!"

Ike looked into Schaulton's eyes, saw the utter craziness, watched him aim the pistol at his face.

The single shot boomed like a cannon.

The back of Stanley Schaulton's skull struck the bay window and fractured it. The man's body was blown flat, covering Ike's.

Ike pushed off the warm corpse and peered into

the woods. Two shapes emerged, but the brilliant sun made it impossible to identify them.

Judy Frymoyer bounded onto the porch, accompanied by a middle-aged, gray haired man. Judy rushed to Ike and took his blood-stained head into her arms. The gray-haired man untied Bertram Hollister, ripped off his shirt and applied pressure to his wound.

Tears streaming down his face, Ike said, "Judy! Oh, Judy! How did you find us?"

"Ike, this is Jeff Palmer," she said, between sobs and amidst tears.

Palmer nodded and said, "As soon as I saw that Stan was wanted by the federal government and was apparently on the run, I realized that Judy's fears were real. I figured he'd come here." Palmer set his thirty ought six on the floorboards. "I guess we got here just in time."

Ike smiled and buried his head in Judy's breasts.

Detective Captain Bertram Hollister lit a Camel.

EPILOGUE

15 August

The small crowd came to attention when the pianist began to play. Bertram Hollister hummed "Here Comes the Bride" with the music. He straightened his tie and turned towards the patio door.

Judge Edgar Frymoyer led his daughter by the arm into Sophie Lepert's rose garden in the walled-in courtyard behind her home. They strolled in time with the music along the white carpet laid on the verdant lawn, and stopped under the flower-laden trellis.

Sophie's garden was gorgeous on this day. Tulips, azaleas, rhododendrons and roses of all colors peppered the green of the grass and the white of the wall. Sophie herself leaned on her walker next to the Reverend and smiled at Ike, who thought that her face looked ten years younger since the day they'd met. He smiled back.

Judy came to his side and squeezed his elbow.

The service was over in ten minutes.

As Ike and Judy kissed, the wedding guests applauded and cheered. Liveried waiters appeared from the house and circulated with trays of champagne in crystal glasses. Toasts were made.

Happy beyond his wildest dreams, Ike led his wife to an empty corner of the courtyard. He sipped his champagne and asked, "How do you feel, Mrs. Darnell?"

Judy laughed. "Oh, Ike, I never thought about that—I guess I'll have to change my name. My patients will get used to it. I love my new name and I love you. I feel wonderful. This is the happiest day of my life. How about you? Pleased with your other decision?"

Ike smiled. "Delighted. I can't wait to get back to taking care of patients. How did you ever get Jeff to arrange for a faculty appointment at Yale?"

"It wasn't hard. Remember, you're one of the most famous Yalies around. You're also one of the most gifted neurosurgeons in the country. Ike, I'm so excited about my new research. Because of you and Natalie Lepert, medical science now has a way to study the immunology of aging. Believe me, it took Yale about two seconds to decide to grab you. It took me less. I'm the luckiest girl on earth."

A brisk, warm breeze whisked through the trees and fields on the banks of the Oswegatchie River and blew suddenly across the courtyard.

Judy studied Ike's handsome face as his eyes watered and his nose ran. He sneezed once, twice, then a third time. Reaching for his handkerchief, he mumbled, "Must be the ragweed."

Judy threw her arms around him. "Oh, Ike, honey. You never told me."

"You never asked."

Judy smiled, kissing him. "There's an awfully good treatment for hay fever," she whispered in his ear.

"Allergy shots?"

Grinning, she nodded.

"I think I'll stick with Benadryl."